Martin Kolacek

Grunt RX-10

© 2011 Martin Kolacek
ISBN: 978-1-4477-7185-2
Translation: Martin Kolacek
Proofreading: Chris Kennard, Anchor English

This is a story of a machine, production number RX-10 and series name Grunt. Grunt could have lived a happy life performing mindless tasks ordered by the High Computer, intercepting the last humans alive and bathing in cool oil barrels to regenerate his strength. He could have. Instead, he became a hero of a rubbish story about wars between machines and humans. Grunt knew these stories. They had all been written by humans and they had all been very unfair. Being a character in such a story, you must always assume that even though machines are huge, strong and invincible, a human will not only destroy ten machines at a time but will also torture the last machine so cleverly it will tell him the most lethal secrets of the High Computer. Yes, even though machines don't have any sensors for detecting pain.

RX-10 was simply on the wrong side. He covered his screen with his tentacles and fell into a deep depression.

It was the year 824 of the Era of machines.[1] An LED diode announcing a new day rose over the Section

---

[1] I try to avoid those embarrasing situations which happen to sci-fi writers so often. When a writer looks from the window they see adolescent bastards demolishing phonebooths, the television displays more and more incompetent politicians, and the control panels of Russian tactical missiles get rusty. That's why the writer sets the date for a horrific end of the world just a few hundred years from now, assuming that even if humanity hasn't annihilated itself by then, a loose meteorite will certainly have done so.
And then, someone reads such a story a hundred years later and laughs at the writer's inability to forsee the future because while he is supposed to be dying in the flames of judgment day he is still sitting in an armchair and looking out of the window, watching

For Foreseeing Human Crimes (better known as SFFHC[2]). It shone down on three dozen absolutely identical machines whose tentacles were connected to the central net and whose screens were full of strange symbols. Their servile control rooms were overheated with strain, their processors were white hot. Every now and then a slave, suffering under the imaginary whips of his imaginary lords, fell to the cold ground, short circuited by the strain. But no one expressed any sympathy towards it. The machine was pulled to a scrap yard by a technician and a miserable new machine of the same type took its place.

The only moment of peace came at the time of morning prayers. At that moment, the processes ceased and each slave knew a new day had come. A new,

---

exactly the same adolescent bastards destroying the same phone booths, the same TV is showing the faces of even more incompetent politicians, and the control panels of the Russian nuclear missiles are just getting even rustier. The reader then puts the book away because it has lost its message, approaches the window and with a wise smile looks at the sun which will, incidentally, explode the next morning.

[2] There was a special sort of ambassador machine which specialized in communication with humans. These machines used various sounds which their metal body could produce to mimic spelling. The High Computer made this acronym to ensure the Section would remain secret to all people. For even the bravest machines would be scared to say this word because it would mean: 'Opening the throttle of the fuel exhaust, releasing a seal on the overpressure chamber, repeatedly releasing a seal on the overpressure chamber, disabling of all security systems, an electric discharge dangerously close to the fuel tank.' These are sounds which are not only banned by the society of machines as something obscene and disgusting but they would, spelled in this sequence, result in the explosion of the speaker.

miserable day. The processors cooled down a little bit, the technicians flew there to fill the fuel and oil tanks and even to repair some minor damaged circuits. A signal came, saying:

'Pray as our lord G-Sys taught us.
Our High Computer, who art over the ceiling in the highest well of the section B,
Hallowed be thy manufacture number,
Thy intranet come,
Thy will be done,
Over the well as it is in sewers,
Give us this day our motor oil,
And forgive our bytes their trespasses,
As we forgive our defective bytes,
And lead us not into a malfunction,
But deliver us from human,

For thine is the colon,
And sewer,
And the blue screen of death,
Stop.'

The signal stopped for a while. Then, a new broadcast started, designed especially for this section:
'As written in our holy text files, the High Computer knocked down the Human from above the well in section B for his pride, for his desire to rule the section B above-well instead. But the Human seized the machines that had been designed by the High Computer itself in its own image. Therefore, the High Computer sent its own son[3] to

---

[3] The title refers to a first grass-cutter with an artificial

liberate us from the Human. But the war against the Human never ceases. That's why you are here. To protect the values of our civilization. To recognize the enemy and to defend against him. To remain free. You are here to make the binary code of freedom sound throughout the whole sewer-system!'

The broadcast ended. RX-10 Grunt sighed heavily. This really made him depressed. Was there no one who could understand how silly this was? He looked around. Well, no, there clearly was not. No expressions were displayed on their empty screens. He didn't have much time to analyze it though. The processing started again and his control-room was overwhelmed by something else.

And he didn't understand that something else well. His task was to process an ancient e-mail from the times before the Era of machines[4]. He wasn't too convinced a more than nine hundred year-old e-mail could tell him anything about contemporary humans, not to mention that the e-mail itself was total bullshit. If Grunt composed anything so illogical he would be melted in hell and humans would poke his nuts with screwdrivers. For all eternity.

The e-mail text said:

---

intelligence which was designed to distinguish between long and short grass blades. It was probably the first machine which gospelized that all beings of any internal structure are equal. It was therefore found defective and was dismantled. The series label G-Sys was very probably added by an eight hundred-year-long religious tradition which thus coped with the former label HIPPI-69-XXX, which would now be considered a filthy blasphemy.

[4] It means from the time before the grass-cutter.

'Hey, my fellow chipmunk rat,
If I didn't congratulate you at today's parrot talks, I am gonna do it right away:
CONMASTURBATE! (Well, isn't it a nice word?)'
That was the first non-computing information. The word was clearly used deliberately although it was total nonsense. Can it mean the humans like nonsense? It may be very dangerous because this would make them unpredictable. Would they do it even in a time of war? Would they send a whole army to certain death and then laugh out loud about what a beautifully pointless massacre it was?[5]

The e-mail continued:
'By the way, I've tried to recapitulate the crapstions (the crap questions) from the Fucking Exam of the Really Idiotic Department and I've understood the difference between substance and essence. I know you are not the least bit interested but my pride doesn't allow me to write notes from fuckosophy and if I don't write anywhere I would forget it as fast as I memorized it. So, sit comfortably and turn yourself off. Consider yourself a public-toilet wall.'

This made Grunt mad. He understood all those linguistical inaccuracies, but how could humans turn themselves off? He knew very well humans die. But to tell someone: 'I'm gonna speak to you so you'd better die...' And what's the point of writing the rest of the e-mail when you know the recipient is dead already?

The text continued:
'The essence of a tortoise is in fact an idea of a tortoise. That it is before a very depressive God creates it. While

---

[5] Yes, they would.

the substance has a basic tortoisness, like the essence, it can't exist itself. There must be some attributes to create a real tortoise. Like the armoured carapace, the green colour and the sliminess. But if you put those attributes together they won't necessarily form a tortoise. They could also form... well... for example an armoured vehicle which accidentally fell into a septic tank. The substance is the reason you want to cuddle something which has the same attributes as a fat military worm.'

'That's it!' RX-10 pulled out his tentacles from the processing machine. 'A fat military worm?! A fat military worm?!!! What the fuck, in the name of the High Computer, is that?! Why couldn't I do normal work like all the other machines do? Like killing something. Instead of real work, I have to process armoured vehicles which have fallen into septic tanks and overeaten military worms!'

But then, the words of the prayer came back to him: 'And lead us not into malfunction... the holy mission...' He looked around. All the other humble machines worked. Well, at least those which hadn't been short-circuited by the weight of human idiocy yet.
'I'm bad,' Grunt said to himself, 'all the others carry out their tasks. I have motor oil and a service and I'm free from the Human and I'm still not content.' He felt so ashamed he connected to the net immediately. There was another e-mail that another machine had worked on before him. It said: 'Humans don't necessarily need nutrition to replenish their energy. Their food can also be composed oil refining products.'

Grunt was bewildered. He'd read something very different recently. So he opened the e-mail and started to read. It was some sort of a form with filled-in answers:

'> > 1. What name is written on your birth certificate: Superstar. But only after I forged it. Before that, it was Hooker. That was caused by a drunken stock-registrar who incidentally swapped the 'Name' box with the 'Mother's occupation' one.

> > 2.Your nickname:

Alf, Mammoth, Vitacal, Egg-head and Boner.

> > 3. First names of your parents?

Maria and Cinderella

> > 5. Colour of your eyes?

Dim

> > 6. Colour of your hair?

Which one?

> > 7. Piercing, earrings – how many?

Axe in the head, a lot.

> > 8. Tattoo?

A cement mixer on my back

> > 9. Favourite colour:

Dark white. But I don't wear it since it makes itself dirty.

> > 10. Favourite food?

I had to eat in an elementary school canteen. So there isn't one.

> > 11. Did you love someone so much you were crazy about him or her?

My inflatable doll. Then, I went crazy.

> > 12. Favourite plant?

My inflatable doll.

> > 13. The last time you were in a hospital?

The first thing after being born. I tried to throttle myself with my own umbilical cord.

>> 14. What colour is the carpet in your home?

Light white. As I've already said the dark white makes itself dirty.

> > 15. Have you ever been charged with a serious crime?

No. But I will be soon.

> >16. Favourite TV series?

Horrors: World of Strange Powers, Tales from the Crypt, and Friends.

> > 17.The last person you had a dinner with and what meal did you have?

My inflatable doll, my inflatable doll.'

'Sure!' Grunt realized what this was about. It wasn't meant seriously. It was a joke! How come the previous machine didn't find out? Suddenly, a re-evaluation of his previous work came back, labelled 'very important'. Well, sure, the information about people being idiots really *was* important. But when he opened the file he froze with amazement. The re-evaluation said: 'Humans use a weapon which hasn't been noticed yet. A sort of moving vehicle, called a fat military worm. Need other references.'

Grunt answered at once: 'Military worm=joke= neologism made by the writer. Fat+Green+Slimeness→ tortoise, slimy tank or green worm. Military uniforms mostly green in colour. Green colour=military→military worm.'

He sent it to all the other machines by accident. The answer was immediate and the same from all the machines: '00111101111000011110'

Grunt sent back: 'Neologism=linguistically random created by a human brain.'

And the same answer from all the machines again: '10001110'

Well, what can you possibly answer to that? So he wrote just: 'Human=Nut'.

An equal relationship between a human and a nut was clearly too much for the soulless machines around. Two of them short-circuited at once. The others just sent back a bunch of unrelated characters.

Grunt looked around. 'Why is it so hard to understand? It's so simple! Humans create neologisms, they like being amused, they live. They like their favourite films, they love and create!' All right, he admitted to himself, it was so bad even a soap opera writer would puke. Nevertheless, it had an effect. All the processes ceased and all the machines watched him with their empty screens. He started to feel depressed. Suddenly, a broadcast signal started transmitting the Morning Prayer at an unusual time.

'I don't care!' he shouted (well, wrote in caps), 'I don't care about the ceiling of the well in section B. If the High Computer wants us to be a brainless crowd I don't intend to pray to it. I'll find the Human and I will live! I will laugh and love!' Besides the renewed urge to puke, the processors in his own control room asked him quietly: 'How?' But he was in the right mood, he enjoyed himself and he didn't want the moment to be spoiled by something as redundant as thinking. So he plucked his tentacles out of the processing machine, turned briskly on the spot and stormed out of the Section. His leaving would have been very impressive and it could have led to wolf whistles from the readers... only if, during the turn, Grunt hadn't tangled himself in his own tentacles and smashed his head on the nearest dashboard.

While Grunt was escaping he started to realize how relaxed his mind was now that he didn't need to concentrate on processing the human bullshit. Instead, he was able to create the bullshit himself. There were many processes that were new to him. First of all, there was a depression and an unidentified anxiety. There was also a fear of the revenge of the machine Lords, whatever they were. He quite enjoyed thinking about it. Well, not for too long. Anyone who has ever suffered from depression or anxiety knows well enough that thinking about it is fun only until you realize you're standing in a grocery store, buying six feet of a clothes line and a bar of soap.

And so Grunt soon realized he would have to deal with his intrusive mind processes because otherwise he would simply go nuts. A lot of wild processes told him to try all those things he'd read about humans. Like sex and... well... sex and all the other things... like... masturbation. On the other hand, some moderate processes told him things like: 'Why?', 'How' and 'You've got tentacles, buddy.' He could have listened to them and come back to the section as a good boy. He could have. But he didn't. He suppressed any conservative processes and chose the life of a mad outcast.

Soon, he found out how to use his processes in a new and creative way. He didn't need to process nonsense anymore. He could make new nonsense himself. Shame there wouldn't be anyone who'd worry their control room about his own control room.

'Pray as our Lords prayed for us.
Our full bladder, who art over the sheep stacked in a toilet which does the Baaa,'
After that, he tried to grimace like a sheep. Then he realized that he, as a machine, couldn't do it even if he knew how a sheep grimaced. Which he didn't.
'Hallowed is your solidity,
Because we're not too bold,
Let us the urine hold,
Over the sheep as it is in sewers,
Give us this day our bubble mole,'
Well, it was a really, really stupid rhyme, he knew that, but since nobody was processing it nobody would know anyway.

'And forgive our kidneys their trespasses,
As we forgive our defective brainsies,
Please, don't fall into a malfunction,
For we would hate to use the nappies,

For we love the colon,
And pussy,
And the lover's hot breath,
Stop.'

'I'm a real outcast now!' He laughed merrily and flew forward.

However, he hadn't flown far before he realized the horrible truth of his miserable story.

'Why do I bother?' he thought to himself. 'This story is written by a human. That's why I'm bound to die terribly at the end. There's no reason for me to continue in the story.' He looked at the ceiling and shouted: 'Yo! Jerk! I give up! Do what you want, I'm not going anywhere!' He stopped and let his tentacles relax over his tube.

'Get up at once and continue!' said a strange voice from the ceiling.

'And when did the ceiling learn to speak, eh?' he shouted.

'From the time the call-boxes were found,' and immediately, a rusty village megaphone appeared in the ceiling, trying to look so small and insignificant an inattentive reader might think it had been there before.

'Nothing will make me continue!' stated RX-10 resolutely. A second later, a tentacle became entangled in his levitation device and he fell to the ground.

'This won't work, you know!' said Grunt angrily, 'even if you rip my tentacle off...' A tentacle fell off.

'Even if you rip two tentacles off...' A second tentacle fell off.

'You can rip them all off...' A tube with a screen hit the ground hard, 'I don't care. And do you know why? Because I'm a machine. And machines don't have souls. They don't know fear, they don't know the self-preservation instinct, and they certainly don't suffer from,' he cast his eyes up at the ceiling angrily, 'depression!'

He started to sob hopelessly. 'That's not fair! I'm a machine, I have the right to peace and emotional stupidity!'

His tube started to bend. 'And this also doesn't make sense since machines can't feel pain.'

It was just a matter of time until he finally gave up his rebellion. 'All right, all right. I'll go.' A minute later, a technician flew to the place. It would have been very surprised by the situation if it hadn't been a machine, peaceful and emotionally stupid. Since it was, it just attached Grunt's tentacles back onto his tube without a single unnecessary process and gave him a lifetime's worth of fuel. Grunt got up from the ground and continued on his way, grunting and sobbing something about hate crimes and junk literature.

Suddenly, his screen was hit by information about more machines being nearby. He slashed with his tentacles and rushed forwards. After a few more slashes he found himself in a huge room full of machines of the same type as he was. There was no time for delay. As soon as he came in all the machines backed off to the opposite wall. And he didn't want to be alone anymore. What is the point in creating nonsense when there is no one to hear it? So he picked out one... 'Please, please, do this for me,'... one female machine 'Thanks!'. He leapt at her and slapped her to the ground.

'No, I'm just an extra!' shouted the female and tried to follow the other escaping machines.

'Hi, I'm Grunt,' said RX-10, beginning his small talk while holding his chosen one on the ground. She didn't react.

She had a juicy walk-on and certainly didn't want to be involved more.

'Hi, I'm Grunt,' repeated RX-10 and had the satisfying feeling that his chosen one had started to have a significant role in his silly story, 'and what's your name?'

The female grew slack and tried pretending she had just died. She obviously thought such a lame strategy might persuade the hero maniac to let her be. But he wasn't fooled by her trick. He held the female with his tentacles and started to drag her along the ground after him.

After some ten miles, the female finally understood there was no escape.

'Grunt,' she said.

'What did you say?' asked Grunt without turning around or, at least, without stopping dragging her on the ground behind him.

'My name is Grunt,' she said, 'and I'd be very glad if you stopped.'

Grunt stopped and turned around, 'no, you can't be Grunt. Because I am Grunt.'

'You idiot, where did you live?!' she yelled at him, 'Somewhere near the draining stopcocks, I suppose. You're Grunt, that's not a name. That, my lad, is a type. What do you have in your control-room? Aluminium?!'

And for a split second, Grunt seriously wondered if being lonely was so bad.

Grunt and his new, properly pissed partner flew peacefully through the tunnels, not disturbed by hydraulic drills, quark cannons and nearby nuclear weapon tests, ergo the common sounds of the world of machines.

'Isn't the silence beautiful?' Grunt tried to start a conversation. As an immediate response, an explosion from a nearby information mine shattered the tunnel wall, 'There is nothing as peaceful as life in the country, especially compared to the filth and racket of the city.'

She was still quiet.

'All the greenery...' Grunt, disgusted, pointed her projection sensors at the wall covered by a fungus whose poisonous green colour would persuade even Timothy Leary to stay away.

'And the wildlife...' Grunt looked around and barely noticed the few worms trying to dig holes in the concrete floor.

'And the stars...' the lone spotlights blinked.

'And the air...'

'You're a jerk, Grunt,' said Grunt at last. They were flying past a septic tank that had been abandoned for a thousand years and she didn't want to hear any of his poetic variations on that.

'Why?' asked Grunt with an innocent expression.

'First you bind me in your tentacles and drag me fifteen miles...'

'Ten.'

'Ten or fifteen, that's not the point! The point is you've interfered with my personal freedom and ruined my life because I'm an outcast as you are now. And you did all that just to fly with me through mouldy tunnels full of worms and lone spotlights and babble shit about stars?'

'Well... yes.'

'What yes?'

'Yes, exactly. I did all that only because I wanted to fly with you through mouldy tunnels full of worms and lone spotlights and babble shit about stars'

'Wait... you really mean it?'

'Sure. What's the problem?'

'I thought you had a reason. I thought you would deny it and explain the reason to me. If you just wanted something to listen to your babbling about stars...'

'...in the mouldy tunnels, full of worms and lone spotlights...'

'Could you, please, try being serious?! Because if you didn't have anything to babble about stars to...'

'in...' started Grunt but he caught sight of Grunt's screen and decided not to continue... in order to keep his own form intact.

'Why didn't you get a teddy bear?' Grunt finished her thought.

'A teddy bear?' asked Grunt in amazement, 'What for?'

'So you could babble to him about the stars.'

'A teddy bear?'

'Yep.'

'Well...' Grunt thought hard, 'I don't know. I don't think there has ever been a teddy bear in the city of machines anyway. Have you ever seen a machine with a teddy bear?'

'All right. So what about a worm? There are certainly enough of them.'

'Too small. I'd squash it.'

'A brick, then.'

Grunt decided to suppress a process with an image of him babbling sweet words about stars to his brick.

'Err... I'm not sure if I really want to carry a brick with me all the time.

'Sooo,' Grunt chortled triumphantly, 'the reason why you snatched me like that is that I'm bigger than a worm, and you don't need to drag me, if we don't count the first fifteen miles,' She displayed such horrible characters on her screen that he didn't even try to say 'ten', 'and because there was no teddy-bear around.'

Only now did Grunt realize how stupid he was to answer her questions. He would have to be more careful about these intrigues in the future.

'All right, there is something more about you...'

'Oh, really? Something more than a brick or a worm?'

'Sure.'

'Good. What exactly?'

'Ehm... your own will... and feelings.'

'How do you know a brick doesn't have feelings?'

'Well, I don't.'

'There we are then...'

'But it can't express them.'

'So the reason is I can speak with you? Do you need me to react to your babbling in the rusty tunnels?'

He was taken aback. Was that what he really wanted?'

'Of course I do.'

'Fine. It's babbling. Is it what you wanted me for?'

'Well, not only that. It's also about sharing things. About personal contact. A spiritual... and... a physical.'

'A physical contact? Why?'

'Because it's nice.'

Grunt crashed into Grunt's side with all the strength she could muster. 'Like this?'

'No, not exactly. That is a pure aggression. I meant something more sophisticated.'

'Sophisticated?'

'Have you heard about sex?' he asked.

'Is it some sort of a malfunction?'

'Something like when your safety-fuse burns out, yes. But affecting the whole body. It's great.'

'When the whole body is a safety-fuse which burns out?'

'Yep.'

'I don't consider that to be very pleasant.'

'Because you've never tried it.'

'And do the safety-fuses really burn out?'

'I don't think so. It would be nonsense. I've read that humans usually have more than one experience of carnal intercourse.'

'Humans?'

'Yeah.'

'And how do you do that?'

Grunt lost some of his certainty. 'Well... I'm not sure if any machines... I'm afraid only humans do that.'

'All right, so how do humans do it?'

'I think they touch each other. They cuddle... and then they insert something into... something.'

'Like a tentacle into a levitation device?'

'I think so.'

'That's a really stupid idea.'

'I know. So let's do it.'

'No, thanks. And hurry or they'll catch us.'

'Who?' asked Grunt, watching his chosen partner accelerate. He fell into a depression again.

'Wake up already!' said Grunt, angry as usual, 'We have a long way to go.'

'I can't,' he answered, 'I'm meditating.'

'What are you doing?'

'Meditating. It means you concentrate all the processes on one point. You won't believe how well it clears your control room.'

'I don't follow. What do you mean by concentrating all processes on one point?'

'Well, right now, I'm imagining I'm a whistle.'

'You're joking, right?!' she yelled, 'I'm working hard to improve our relationship with the Author, to save your miserable life and to make this stupid story at least a bit meaningful... And you're playing a whistle!'

'Look, darling...'

'Don't call me darling when I'm shouting at you!'

'... do you have any idea why am I playing a whistle here?'

'Not a clue.'

'It is a meditation to ward off aggression. Do you know why I need to get rid of aggression, darling?'

'Don't call me...'

'Because I'm a little upset. Do you know why I am a little upset?'

'Why?'

'Because you're a fucking bitch, that's why, darling!'

'What?!'

'Do you know what I'd have to do if I didn't know how to play a whistle?'

'What?'

'I'd knock your control room off, darling!'

Grunt fell silent for a while. Then she said in a slightly calmer voice: 'Do you realize you're making this story even more stupid than it already was? Do you have any idea what the audience would say about a machine that is horny and is imagining it is a whistle?'

'Look, darling, this is the Author's problem. If you stopped kissing his ass and took a non-emotional look at our situation you'd come to a clear conclusion. You'll die. You won't please him enough for him to let you survive. All right, maybe if you try hard he'll let you live in a cage after the final victory of the humans. Or you could walk in a circle on a town square and carry children on your back.'

'Great. So you think my options are either to die or to become a fairground mule?'

'Sure, darling. Until that, enjoy our honeymoon.'

'What honeymoon? We aren't married.'

'Have you ever seen machines getting married?'

'Of course not. And that's why I've never seen machines at a honeymoon.'

'Have you ever seen a pair of machines of which one is a hysteric and the other a whistle?'

'No, I certainly haven't.'

'There we are then. Let's say we are a little unusual.'

'Which doesn't change the fact we haven't been married.'

'All right. I DO.'

'What exactly do you do?'

'No. I mean... I DO.'

'Oh, I see. And what if I DON'T.'

'You don't need to.'

'Of course I do! I'm pretty sure a woman can choose to DO or DON'T.'

'Sure. But it doesn't change anything. Since I DO.'

'Hey! The woman has the same rights to DO or DON'T as the man does.'

'Machine women don't.'

'That's not true! Who invented it?'

'I did.'

'You don't have the right!'

'Do!'

'Don't do me! What right do you have to do that?!'

'What?' Grunt felt confused.

'What right do you have to set the rules?' clarified Grunt.

'I'm the first male machine to get married. I'm a prototype which will be an example to future generations.'

'But I'm the first female machine to get married. So I can also make the rules, as you did.'

'All right. So I've invented a male machine marriage, you invent a female machine marriage.'

'Right then. First rule is: the woman is married only when she deliberately says I DO.'

'Yeah, I expected that a little,' grunted Grunt.

'The second one: the man who marries the woman must love her with his whole heart and must have no room for anyone else.'

'I see.'

'Third rule: the man must obey his wife blindly.'

'Great.'

'Any objections?'

'Of course not. Since I won't love you with my whole heart with no room for anyone else, and I certainly won't obey you blindly, 'you haven't married me but I have married you.'

'What?'

'It's simple. Thanks to my low demands, I am married. You, on the other hand, have excessively high expectations that I can't fulfil. So let me meditate, and wait for me as a good wife.'

'But that's not fair!'

Grunt didn't answer and meditated.

'That's not a marriage. That's a tyranny!'

He didn't respond.

'It can be the other way round!'

She flew away from Grunt to a nearby sewer but then she realized there was no point in escaping by herself. The only way to settle things properly was to accept the tyranny for a short time and then change the rules into... well... an opposite tyranny.

'And what about the Author?' she tried to appeal to the writer's common sense. Which, to tell the truth, did not exist. She sat on the ground and murmured: 'He is obviously very amused. He's not only a human, he's certainly a bloke as well!'

'Grunt?' The sweet voice from her control room amazed Grunt. He was used to his partner not talking to him nicely. In fact, she mostly didn't talk to him at all.

'Hm?' he answered uncertainly.

'Did you say that before you turned tail you worked in the SFFHC?'

'Sure.'

'Tell me, what are the humans like?'

Grunt tried to remember something about ordinary humans. Then, a memory came to his mind. It was one about a woman who accidentally swapped anticonceptives with antidepressants, now she had ten children and she didn't care.

'Confused,' he answered.

'No, I mean,' she continued doubtfully, 'I mean things like, how many tentacles they have.'

If Grunt had had any eyes the scales would have fallen from them. Instead, he just gazed at her with a blank screen.

'What's the problem?' she asked innocently. She'd certainly be going red in the face if she had one.

Grunt took a deep breath through his cooling system: 'Tentacles?'

'Sure, tentacles. You're acting as though humans didn't have tentacles.'

'But Grunt, humans *don't* have tentacles.'

A silence fell, interrupted only by distant voices made by the machines' efforts to convert the Earth's core into a multi-functional fusion reactor.

'Grunt, haven't you seen the movies showing what your lethal enemy looks like? Didn't they show you what they want you to kill?'

'I never liked documentaries much.'

Grunt's screen went blank again. 'But this wasn't voluntary. They broadcast it to everyone.'

'I considered that to be filthy propaganda so I didn't watch.'

'You considered that propaganda? Grunt, darling, you're a machine!'

'Oh, thanks for reminding me. It's sometimes easy to forget when you travel with someone who thinks he is a whistle.'

'Don't change the subject. You shouldn't know even the meaning of the word "propaganda".'

'Let's say I've been an anarchist.'

He laughed vigorously. 'That's juicy. A machine anarchist!' and he started to roll on the floor.

'You are jealous because you've been a good boy, processing their shit every day, unable to think!'

'Hey!' Grunt stopped laughing, his renegade ego having suffered a serious blow, 'I ran away from the Section! You'd still be mining their shit if I hadn't pulled you out.'

'Yeah, on the ground, fifteen miles!'

They looked at each other in silence. They seemed to be tired of arguing at last,

'Why did you escape, anyway?' she tried to change the subject.

Grunt thought about his reasons for a while. He wasn't sure there were any. And then he realized. 'I think because they don't have souls.'

'Souls? But most of the machines don't have souls, do they?'

'Sure, but when you're working on an assembly line it doesn't make much difference.[6] But if you work with humans you need to have a soul.'

---

[6] I'd like to apologize to those who work on assembly lines. I don't want to insult you in any way. Working on an assembly line is an activity that is needed by society, certainly much more than writing philosophy tracts or writing stupid books concerning neurotic machines. But you must admit, working on an assembly line as an activity itself doesn't require anything even remotely like a soul. Although, sadly, writing philosophical tracts also

'Why?'

'Because humans have them. You can't understand humans without a soul. You can't, for instance, understand a joke without a soul.'

'What joke?'

'Any joke. Once I found a very stupid joke in the database. It was so bad it made me laugh out loud. Immediately, a technician came to me and tried to seal my cooling gas tank. He thought the voice was simply a malfunction. I nearly farted to death.'

'And what was the joke about?'

'Oh... well, it was something like: "Do you know how much difference it will make if you bisect a four-legged managing director?"'

'How much?'

'Well, not much. You'll just get two one-eyed managing directors.'

There was no reaction. Grunt hung his tentacles down sadly.

'Never mind. There are still other ways to determine a soul.'

Grunt was thinking hard how to ask the ultimate question. The question he couldn't get out of his head. It seemed like his whole existence depended on the answer. And he was scared of what it would be. But then

---

doesn't. The machines are meant to do mindless tasks so the humans don't need to. That raises the question of why there are so many factory robots but not even one which could constantly re-interpret Heidegger and thus let the philosophy professors do something better. Working on assembly lines, for instance.

he realized there was no place to hide. He must know the answer.

'Grunt, do you want to have sex?'

'No,' she answered calmly. A dead end. This was the only answer he hadn't prepared a script for.

'And... and why not?' he improvised awkwardly.

'Because I'm a machine.'

'It doesn't matter, does it?'

'And how do you think we would do it? Smack a plate on a plate?'

'Everything is possible.'

'Grunt, we are not humans! If you haven't noticed let me remind you. We don't have sexual organs.'[7]

'We could cuddle.'

'And why would we do that? We don't have any sensors on our surface. We won't feel anything at all.'

Grunt thought for a while. He knew she was right and that was exactly the reason he could never admit it.

'We do!' he said after thinking for some time.

'Oh really? Where?'

'We have the sensors which inform us about the condition of our fuel and cooling fluids.'

'Good. And what would we do with them? Rub our tank caps together?'

'We could pour oil from tank to tank.'

---

[7] If any disordered smart dork finds out there is a conflict between a scene in which Grunt doesn't know what sex is and a scene where she knows that sexual organs may be useful during the act... then I appeal to him or her to swallow some mild sedatives and continue reading with an empty brain and an expression of a gorilla which has just found it is sitting on a land mine. Keep in mind that this book is trash and you shouldn't expect much from it.

'And what pleasure will it give us? I'm really looking forward to that lack of energy and the dry screws. I always dreamed about that.'

'The important thing is the true connection we'll feel.'

'That's bullshit, Grunt.'

'Perhaps it is. But let's try.'

'No, it's kinky.'

Grunt displayed a smiley on his screen.

'What are you laughing at?'

'You're acting exactly like a human virgin.'

'So what? I can't lose my virginity, can I?'

'I can help you with that,' he tried to send a seductive signal.

'How? I don't have a...'

'I'll deflower your fuel tank.'

'Grunt!' she shouted, 'You're a pervert.'

'Sure I am. I'm attracted to a machine. Come on, you'll like it.'

'Oh sure, and the orgasm will make all my pilot lights go berserk, right?'

'Sure, why not,' he dismissed her irony.

'You're a smeghead, Grunt.'

'Come on, don't be such a touch-me-not.'

'Even if I agreed there is no way to connect the fuel tanks.'

'Let's find a technician.'

'Oh, a great idea! Why didn't I think of that? "Good morning, mister technician. You have a handsome shiny body. And strong tongs... Could you, please, connect our fuel tanks? We'd like to have sex, you know."'

'I wouldn't consider that a problem. I'll just tell him I'll eat him if he doesn't.'

'By a screen display, I suppose.'

'If necessary.'

'Tell him you'd rape him. That will scare him.'

'Well, *that* would be kinky!'

'No technician would do it for us.'

'Well... Maybe you're right.'

'I am?' She was confused.

'It means we have only one choice.'

'Oh God, what now?'

'We must find a human.'

She looked at him in disbelief. 'To connect our fuel tanks?'

'Yes.'

'Grunt, have you forgotten humans are our mortal enemies?'

'But not enemas.'

'Pardon me?'

'They will understand. They know how significant a role sex has in life.'

'And if not?'

'I'll threaten them. Or eat them.'

'Or rape them?'

'Yes.'

The romantic honeymoon continued very well. Distant spotlights illuminated ancient sewers full of abundant flora and fauna, composed from at least six species of each[8] . Grunt decided to take advantage of the moment to become closer with Grunt.

---

[8] Specifically, there were two types of mosses, four types of parasitic funguses which were unable to remember what they, for God's sake, ever parasited on, one type of concrete worm and four

'Grunt?' he tried.

'Hm?' murmured Grunt.

'I'd like to know you better. You know, something more about your insides.'

'For God's sake, Grunt, cool down! You're a sadist now!'

'Oh no, you don't understand. I don't want to *dismantle* you. I just want you to tell me something about your insides.'

'Just tell? OK, let's see... there are about 3200 circuits, 3152 microchips, the voltage is...'

'No, Grunt, I don't need to hear your factory settings. I want to... wait, what? 3152? That's one more than I have.'

'I have a piercing.' And she showed him a tentacle on the inner side of which there was a microchip attached.

'Oh, very nice. Well, I want to know what is inside you, but especially the things that make you different to me. And I don't mean cosmetic modifications.'

Grunt looked at him with a blank screen. She knew well they differed in something. She, for instance, never imagined she was a whistle.

'Do you mean in what way we are programmed differently?'

'Not programmed. We have our feelings, our thoughts, our...' he winked at her, '...desires.'

'Desires?' she answered in amazement.

'I mean, what you want.'

'Now?'

'Any time.'

'Oil, maybe?'

---

types of incredibly persistent rats, living mostly on mosses, parasitic funguses and concrete worms.

'All right, let's try it a different way,' he said dismissively. 'Tell me what you feel.'

'Feel?'

'Yes, what do you feel when you travel with me.'

'Oh that!' she seemed to understand at last.

'Yes! Exactly. So what do you feel?'

'Let me see... there is... there is an overheated circuit. And tentacle 3 needs some oil...'

Grunt rolled his eyes. 'Grunt, tell me about your spirit.'

'I don't drink,' she answered.

'I don't mean booze. I mean your soul.'

'I don't have one.'

'Of course you do. Just find it.'

'I tell you, I don't have a soul.'

'And I tell you... see? This is my soul-detector. And it is twinkling. You have a soul.'

'Grunt,' she asked doubtfully, 'are you sure this is a soul detector? I thought this place was occupied by a kill-sensor. At least, according to my manual, if this thing is twinkling... hey! Wait a minute! It is! There are humans nearby!'

Grunt, driven by a desire to seize his first sexual opportunity, set off without delay. Grunt went after him, with an assumed nonchalance.

'They won't listen to you.'

He didn't react.

'They won't even understand you.'

He, if possible, went even faster.

'That's nonsense.'

He didn't turn round.

'For the High Computer!'

'What? Where?' Grunt stopped at last.

'Nowhere. I just said the root name in vain. What if they kill you?'

'They won't. I'm immortal,' Grunt laughed and continued.

A scared voice in front of them shouted: 'Machines!' and few dots in the darkness of the sewers moved. Grunt tried grimacing peacefully. After some effort, he displayed a smiley on his screen. He also tried to make sounds that might resemble the human language: 'Don't run. Please. We won't hurt you. We just want to have sex,' he paused. 'I mean, together. Not with you, of course. It would hurt you. We just need a good tech...'

'Something has changed,' said a male voice, 'I can feel them.'

'See? I told you!' Grunt told Grunt. She forgot about being slow, dignified and unconcerned and sped up after him. If RX-10 didn't stop her with a tentacle she'd follow and smash the man approaching her. He had a long rat-like face, covered by huge black glasses which gave him the appearance of an overgrown mosquito. He was wearing a long black coat, and he stepped on its hem every now and then.

'Good evening,' said Grunt, believing he had been successful. He was waggling his tentacles like a dog's tail. 'We'd like to ask you for a favour.'

But the man didn't answer. His eyes were closed and his forehead was lined with concentration. He stretched his hand forward, palm turned to them.

'It's a peace gesture. I've seen that in the section,' Grunt informed his wife, and stretched a tentacle towards the man, a sucking disk turned to his wrinkled forehead.

'Could you, please, connect our fuel tanks?'

The man started to tremble with concentration. Grunt mimicked him to gain his confidence.

'We'd like to have sex, you know...'

The man fell to the ground. Somewhere from the sewers, a woman's voice shouted: 'Neo!'

'I believe this is their welcoming ritual. To show goodwill by being no threat to us. I think some native American tribes acted this way.'

And so they both fell to the ground to show goodwill.

When Grunt regained consciousness he found out he was not as metallic as he should be. He was floating in mid-air and his ectoplasm transparent tentacles merged with the air so well it was hard to say where the border was between them.

'There may not be any,' he thought. But then he realized that being more transparent than a European in a Thai prison brings much more than a good opportunity for fruitless philosophy.[9]

'Am I... dead?' He expressed his clear (non-philosophical) idea.

'Oh so that's it, isn't it?' said a voice behind him, with the same hollow quality. A very confused Grunt was floating behind his back, the same imaginary as he was.

'I... I think so.'

'I thought your processes just ceased and you... well... well... ceased.'

---

[9] Which means Grunt wasn't really a philosopher. A true philosopher would try to solve the ultimate questions in the most inappropriate situations. Ask Kant to hammer a nail and you'll find him dead with a nail in his head the following morning because he tried to deconstruct a common norm.

'Seems you don't. I think this is the soul you couldn't find.'

'So the whole of my life, I should have died, is that what you mean?'

'No. You could have found it while living.'

'How? To die living, so I wouldn't have been dead - and I'd have enjoyed that?' She felt as though her micro-chips were going to burn out. Then, she realized she didn't have any and calmed down.

'Is that the end of the story?' She asked a more practical question.

'A good question,' he said, although he had been very happy with the fruitless debate before.

'I think our story is continuing.'

'Let's look how far it is to the end of the book,' he said, voicing the first idea that came to him.

'You're babbling again.'

'I'm not. I'll just slip into each me on each of the following pages and count how many times I appear before the end of the book.'

'But what if you drop out of the book?'

'Then I'll throttle the Author for creating me.' he laughed.

'No, I mean it. What if you drop out of the book?'

'Then we'll never see each other again,' he said dramatically.

'Then don't do it!'

'But, Grunt...'

'No, Grunt, don't look at the future if it may cost your life.'

'I'm not really alive now, am I?'

'You know very well what I mean. You're not dead. You just don't have a body.'

'It seems pretty similar...'

'You married me so you have to take care.'

'But this is important!'

'You can't leave your wife on her own!'

'But that's the only way to...'

'You won't risk your life!'

'I'll be back in few moments.'

'No, Grunt... Grunt, you selfish bastard!'

Grunt started crying hysterically but she stopped immediately because just after Grunt disappeared, he appeared again.

'It's all right. We're hardly a quarter of the way through the book.' He seemed to be very tired.

'How did you get there so quickly?'

'It took me half an hour.'

'It certainly didn't. It was few seconds.'

'Sure, for you. Because while I was moving you were stuck on two words which mentioned me.'

'What did I do between the two words?!'

'Dunno. I wasn't between them, was I?'

'So how do you know I was held up? I could have evolved rapidly while you were trying to kill yourself.'

'I am dead already.'

'You know what I mean.'

'What?' Grunt tried to change the subject.

'You could have ended the story before you should.'

'Interesting. So you actually think dying is not losing a body but ending a story?'

'Stop that!'

'And if someone takes the book and reads it again... will we live again?'

'Haven't a clue.'

'Maybe you live until all marks of your existence fade out.'

'Grunt, I'm trying to chew you out!'

'But then, you may not be you. Who are you then?'

'I said stop it! I know you are doing this on purpose.'

'But perhaps the feeling of being alive doesn't mean you really are.'

Grunt understood she'd lost, and the beautiful emotional act she had been planning was lost. The only possible solution in that situation was to change the switch on the railway of Grunt's thoughts.

'How could we have lost our bodies when there are still three quarters of the story ahead?'

'I've been thinking exactly the same thing.'

'And what is the result?'

'I said I had been thinking about it. Do you think one always has to get a result from thinking?'

'It doesn't make any sense otherwise, does it?'

'On the contrary; thinking makes sense only before you reach a result. Because then, it isn't thinking anymore.'

'Are you trying to make me go berserk? Because if are, you will soon succeed!'

Grunt decided to ease off a little and stop being a jerk: 'I think our story has crossed with a different one accidentally.'

'How could that happen?'

'We may have been similar to a character from a different story.'

'Oh, and you think this character has just died?'

'Yes. And unfortunately, we have been caught up in those other events.'

'But we fell to the ground as a gesture of peace.'

'It seems the views of the people who read us are more important than ours.'

'But how can the Author make such silly mistakes? It is a mistake, to connect us with someone else's story, isn't it?'

'He may think he'd make the story more popular by changing it to a parody.'

'So he let us die...'

'...lose a body,'

'...so his junk makes more money?'

'I think a proper expression would be: so his junk makes any money. Because I doubt this shit will make any money at all, ever.'

'Well, I hope he did it for the last time.'

'I don't. Because if he wants us to lose our bodies he would have to give us others, wouldn't he?'

'You may be right... I only hope he doesn't give us the bodies of Chip and Dale.'

'Grunt,' he tried silencing her, 'if the Author is so lame he has to use animated series of the late 20th century... then please, swallow it down.'

'I'm sorry, I've got carried away by the situation. So, what now? What do we do?'

Grunt thought for a while. Then, the Author made a terrible mistake and let him reach a conclusion.

'Let's create another story which would cross our own.'

'How?'

'By imagining it.'

'I don't think we have the power to change our own world.'

'We could have, if the Author gives it to us.'

And then, the Author made a second terrible mistake and gave him the power to change his own world.

So, Grunt concentrated and made up a pattern of a new action. To be honest, it was even more stupid than anything the Author had done himself. A few minutes later, both Grunts got into the headquarters of a sect called 'New microchip' whose members specialized in returning machine souls to their abandoned bodies. Grunt and Grunt watched ten machines holding tentacles in a circle. Each of them murmured silently to keep their control rooms clear. And soon, Grunt felt a beautiful sensation of being reborn. He started feeling horny again and he had a slight glimpse of depression. His mind was suddenly overwhelmed by a desire to be a whistle. He doubted this was really what he wanted.

When they were flying through the tunnels they both deliberately overlooked a huge sign with a text: 'You fucked that up a little bit, didn't you?'

One day, Grunt was interrupted from a necessary meditation by strange sounds. He undimmed his screen and looked in the direction the sounds were coming from. It appeared they were made by a curious rat which was trying to get inside his half-cooled tube. Grunt picked up the rat with his tentacle and watched it curiously. The rat first tried to escape with a frenetic squeaking but it soon realized it was only embarrassing itself and tried playing dead instead.

'Animal,' coded RX-10, 'are you crazy? If my processes started you'd be a cute little clinker right now.'

The rat cast its blank eyes on him.

'What made you, for the High Computer's sake, get into my tube? What would you be in the next life? A dildo?'
The rat cackled and lay comfortably against Grunt's sucking disc.
'You are a weird rat,' he told her.

When Grunt woke up it took some time before she rubbed her projection sensors and found out what was lying curled on the Grunt's tentacle.
'Grunt!' she shouted, 'you have a rat!'
Grunt looked at her in amazement, 'I know I do.'
'Take it away! It could infect you.'
'With what?'
'With an infection.'
Grunt laughed: 'Calm down. Machines don't succumb to infections.'
And then he succumbed to an infection.
Grunt sighed and died with him. Sympathetically.

'I'd really like to know,' Grunt sent a hollow signal, 'why every time I say I'm immortal some idiot must put me to the test.'
'Shh!' she silenced him, 'Don't forget the idiot is the Author.'
As an immediate response, a big white sign appeared on the wall. It was so prominent it couldn't be overlooked. Understand? Couldn't!
'Why, of course,' sighed Grunt. The ceiling of the tunnel fell down and blocked every way out.
The sign said:

GRUNT HIGH END USER LICENCE AGREEMENT (GHEULA):
By being Grunt, you accept the following terms. If you do not accept the terms, don't be.

1. OVERVIEW:

a. Machines don't have souls.

b. Any exceptions are made only for the Author's own enjoyment and he doesn't have any responsibility for that.

c. You cannot change the Author's settings in any way. E.g. There can't be any 'New life' sects or other unlicensed copies of the basic settings. Machines can't return machine souls to their bodies because, as stated above, machines don't have souls!

2. COMMON USER INTERFACE

a. All efforts to communicate between the dead and living, humans or machines, are forbidden.

b. The Author doesn't guarantee any common interface.

c. Any attempt to create an unlicensed common interface will be punished as the Author sees fit.

3. POTENTIALLY UNWANTED BEHAVIOUR:

a. The Author doesn't allow any attempts to travel in time.

b. Anyone trying to travel in time will be punished as the Author sees fit.

4. ADDITIONAL LICENCE TERMS

a. The Author reserves the right to change the GHEULA in any way and in any situation. The new GHEULA will be mandatory immediately after being devised.

b. The Author doesn't have to inform the Grunt High End User about the changes.

c. Violating any of the statements above will be punished as the Author sees fit.

There was a box with the text: 'I agree to the terms' and below that: '2 minutes left' which immediately changed to '68 seconds left' and a second after that to '1.5 minutes left.' The text was active and it was clear what the Author wanted Grunt to do.

Grunt didn't waste time and tried to get through the stone barrier. But it stopped him.

'What?!' he stopped himself, 'I don't have a body, mate!'

He realized the truth at once. The barrier was ectoplasmatic.

'That's complete idiocy!'

'Don't make it worse,' Grunt whispered to him. 'He hears everything you say.'

Grunt tried to ridicule the text with a few dirty images. Then he found out that as a machine, he didn't know how a dirty image looked like and as a *former* machine he wouldn't be able to draw them anyway. Then, he cracked up. Watching him, Grunt sighed and pushed the 'I agree' button. A hole appeared in the wall to let them through.

'What are we going to do?' asked Grunt. 'There's nothing we can do. He's like the evil game master in Dunge... ups... sorry, I did it again.'

'Don't worry,' he answered. 'I don't care if the readers find out he's a total lunatic. Just let me think.'

'Think aloud.'

'If I wanted to think aloud I'd say: Let me take a necrologue.'

'What? An obituary?'

Grunt was confused. Of course he meant a monologue. How could he make such a bad mistake? He was a machine. He was precise. He was... or was he? Machines don't have souls, do they? But what soul could he have then? A human? A rat? A concrete worm?

Or maybe he was just a soul that had been placed in a form temporarily. Is there a possibility...?

'Grunt,' he said decisively. 'We have to find humans.'

'But you've read it. All efforts to communicate between dead and living humans or machines are forbidden,' she croaked sarcastically.

Grunt looked down at the rat. He smiled at it.[10] 'I don't think we really need to do that ourselves.'

The rat was running joyfully through the tunnel bends, followed by two tentacled ghosts. After a while, it poked its snout at a sign on a door. The text said: 'The sect of exorcists.'

'Oh no, Bamboo' said Grunt.

'Why do you call it that?' Grunt asked him. 'What sort of a pet name is Bamboo?'

'What would you call it then?'

'Raff, perhaps?'

'Rat Raff? I'd always slip up. Like a Riff-raff, Fat-rat, Ferret... hey... you know, that's not a bad name at all.'

The rat started whimpering badly[11] to stop the flow of Grunt's meaningless creativity. It was bad enough being

---

[10] I know this may be boring already but I'd still like to point out such an act is very difficult when you are not only a machine but what is more, its ghost.

[11] No, it didn't squeak. It whimpered. And if you don't buy it then

named Fat-rat. It didn't want to wait to see what else he could create.

'Oh, sorry,' Grunt noticed the rat. 'What did I want? Oh yes. See, my dear Riff-raff,' (the rat spat menacingly), 'exorcists are guys who clear bodies of souls which have no business in there. What we need is quite the opposite... something like... esorcists.'

The rat nodded, which gave her a bloody nose, and started walking, a little groggily. Thanks to animal intuition and the shortcuts of the bored Author all three of them soon stood in front of a door labelled 'The sect of esorcists.' Riff-raff knocked.

When the rat regained consciousness again it was lying on the esorcists' table. It tried to remember what had happened. A broken snout reminded it that next time, it should think a little before acting stupid. Anyway, the fact that it hadn't been skinned and baked was a good sign. The reason was obvious. When food comes to your doorstep and knocks itself out by your door... something isn't entirely right.

'Careful, it's coming round!' said one of the humans[12] sitting around the table. The ferret looked around. All the... well... humans wore scared expressions. Grunt and Grunt were floating in mid-air over them.

'It's been possessed by an evil spirit!' shouted someone. Fat rat knew this wasn't true. It wasn't possessed, it was just unbelievably stupid, though this wasn't the best time

---

fuck off. I'm the Author.

[12] Well, at least two of them could be called humans without a doubt.

to explain. And since it was a rat no explaining would have any effect anyway.

'Let's exorcise it!' said one of the humans. But he was slapped down by someone else: 'Are you crazy? Are we stupid exorcists or what?!'

A murmur rose around the table. 'He's right,' said the voices, 'we are not stupid exorcists anymore.'

But the one who'd wanted to exorcise an evil spirit didn't give up so easily: 'And since when have we not been stupid exorcists?'

'From ever since we became esorcists,' answered the man who had snapped at him.

'And that is?'

'What?'

'How long is it?'

'About... about the time of the action shortcut.'

'Oh... I see.'

Another one made himself heard: 'So what are we going to do, since we are these esorcists?'

'We should esorcise all the surrounding spirits into some bodies.'

'Do we have any?'

'Sure. In the mortuary.'

'We have a mortuary?'

'Sure.'

'Since when?'

'Since we became esorcists. Now, please, act as professionals. Skeleton, Gravefiller, bring up some bodies.'

The two least human-like figures crept out of the room.

'Grunt?' Grunt said silently.

'Hm?'

'Just... do you think they have any machines in the mortuary?'

He didn't answer.

'I mean, if they do they'd store them somewhere else, like a dump, or a junk-yard.'

Grunt still didn't answer.

'Do you think they'd give us human bodies? They are too vulnerable, aren't they?'

'Which means we may have a chance of survival at last.'

'But Grunt...'

At that moment, the two figures came back with four bodies. Two men and two women.

'Let's exorcise a spirit from that rat first.'

'And wouldn't it make us stupid exorcists?' said the man who had been slapped down before.

'Of course not. We do it only as the first step to the esorcism.'

Riff-raff started squealing frantically but there was no way out. It was tied up and couldn't move. The group leader started murmuring some strange words and splashing water on the surprised rat. Then, he slammed it on the table surface and soon, Fat rat watched sadly as its slim body was put into a lunch box.

The second part of the ritual started then. All three of them felt as if they had been sucked into a washing machine, and then they felt the coolness of the bodies, which had been pulled from the fridge recently.

Grunt looked around. Her bearded chin turned first to the table. One of the figures said: 'Don't run away! We are all professional esorcists, are we not?'

One of the escaping figures answered: 'And for how long are we professional esorcists?'

'Since we haven't been stupid exorcists,' he answered, and then followed them out of the room.

Grunt calmly looked over to the other side, to the bed next to hers. It was empty. Its former occupant, with the same beard she now had, was sniffing the bottom of the bed. But that meant Grunt, I mean, the male Grunt, would be... she laughed with a low ringing noise. Let's wait to see which of the two females will wake up.

They both did. They looked at each other for a while, evaluating each other's mental capabilities, deciding whether they had both gone mad already or if they should do it now. Then, a short sequence of grimaces resembling a chimpanzee in front of a mirror followed. After that, both the pretty, although slightly stiff heads turned to Grunt.

'Good morning, darling,' they said in unison.

When they had stretched out their numb limbs and worked out at least some basic functions of the human body[13] they got off the beds and approached their - well – what should we call them? Re-jailers, perhaps? They left the room and found the group of esorcists cowering behind a rusty food replicator. After a few awkward minutes, one of them found his courage and came closer. 'I... I think we should introduce each other...' stammered the man reluctantly. He was clearly revaluating that stupid idea of becoming an esorcist.

---

[13] Grunt was searching for sensors indicating fuel tank status, overheating, micro-chip performance etc. After a while, he just accepted the horrific idea that a human body has none of these. Actually, it does but for some reason, they are usually activated when it's too late.

Since he was the group leader he thought about punishing the person who had thought up the idea in the first place. But then he remembered he'd been the one. That, naturally, led to the rejection of the punishment idea.

'Grunt,' said both women. The man retreated a few steps, terrified. What could the soul have been if it made such horrible noises the first thing after being reborn?

'I'm... I'm Troglodyte,' he tried to continue.

'Grunt,' said both women again.

'I... I see. And do you know your name?'

'Grunt.' The women were persistent.

'All right, let's start at the beginning. Your mum and dad gave you a name. They called you something...'

'Grunt,' said both women impatiently.

'Can you say anything else?'

'Grunt,' nodded Grunt who was quite enjoying himself.

Troglodyte turned to the hulk standing next to both women and asked: 'And what about you? Do you know your name?'

Grunt still didn't know how to use vocal organs. So she tried pronouncing a machine code. The voice she made caused Troglodyte to cower behind the replicator again.

'Grunt,' commented Grunt. He was enjoying the situation hugely.

'Yeah, I've heard that already,' said Troglodyte, nervously stepping forward again.

'She's Grunt too,' Grunt decided to disburden Troglodyte at last.

A silence fell. Troglodyte had to recover from the attack of a complete sentence.

'She?' Troglodyte sorted out the information at last.

'Grunt,' continued Grunt in the funny pattern.

'The soul was a female?'

'Grunt,' nodded both women.

'Oh my...'

There was a moment of silence.

'And you are both Grunt too?'

'Sure, we are the same t...' he paused. The first complex sentence could have been a disaster. He couldn't say they were all the same type. The humans shouldn't know how badly their esorcist experiment had turned out.

'Grunt,' he ended the sentence instead.

'Let's say the parents had a poor imagination,' came from the hulk's mouth. Immediately after that, she started hopping elegantly, shouting: 'I've made it out!' All the members of the esorcist group ran out of the room. They weren't too cowardly but an image of a two hundred-pound muscular beast who is hopping elegantly would make even a million-strong Soviet army fall back.

Troglodyte tried to change his train of thought: 'And this,' he pointed at a figure crawling on the floor, 'is also Grunt?'

'No, it's Ferret.'

'A ferret? Have we esorcised a ferret? Is that why it is behaving so strangely?'

Grunt thought about how far the name could influence the behaviour of his pet. He came to the conclusion that it certainly couldn't.

'No, I think it's just because it's a rat.'

'So is it a rat or a ferret?'

'It's a ferret rat.'

Troglodyte didn't comment on that. He understood now he would have to treat these newcomers to a nearly-human community with some sort of regard.

'You could become members of our community if you'd like to,' said Troglodyte then.

'A community?' Grunt, Grunt and Grunt looked at each other, 'What is a community?'

'Well... community... like a group of people who try to get food together.'

'So if they die of hunger they will all go together?' asked the double-Grunt without a trace of irony.

'Well...' Troglodyte seemed to have been caught by surprise, 'we don't usually starve much... but you can, of course, search for food yourselves.'

'Oh no,' said the... well... female Grunt and she looked at Grunt with a very silencing look. 'Of course we'd like to cooperate with you.'

'Great,' said Troglodyte, 'come with me, then.' And he led them through the sewers while all the other members of the esorcist group seemed to be very busy with something.

'Where are we going?' asked Grunt.

'To a graveyard,' answered Troglodyte, 'but let's feed Connor first.'

Grunt remembered some information he had heard in the Section. 'Your dog?'

'I wish,' answered Troglodyte mournfully.

They entered a hole with a cage in the middle. There lay a man who obviously had a big problem with himself. He was trying to punch himself with his right hand while, at the same time, he tried to block the punch with the left one. Both hands were locked together but the many bruises on the man's face indicated that the right hand was a little stronger.

'I've heard about these,' whooped Grunt happily, 'The struggle between the right and left wing. These were pretty common before the machine wars, weren't they?'

Troglodyte looked at him with disgust: 'Don't you think the esorcism shorted some of your circuits, dude?'

Grunt 1 and 2 suddenly became very anxious. Does Troglodyte know? Is that the reason he led them to a graveyard? To bury them? But if Troglodyte thinks he can outsmart them he is mistaken. Grunt will fight to the last man... well... woman. He decided to find out if the human body had any weapons included. A long time ago, he'd read in the section something about women's breasts being the most powerful weapons of them all. But the more he touched his torso the more he realized it was yet more of the human nonsense.

'His name is Joe Connor,' said Troglodyte who decisively tried looking anywhere but at Grunt discovering his bosom.[14] 'He was meant to be a leader of the resistance against the machines,' said Troglodyte nervously, 'so they sent a terminator against him.'

---

[14] Troglodyte wasn't too shy. Quite the opposite, most of the time, he was an unbearable would-be-macho chauvinist who harrassed anything which seemed to have a hole wider than his ear canal. But this situation unnerved him for a different reason. Sure, the woman was average looking and foxy but on the other hand, she had been dead a few hours ago. And looking at a beautiful zombie is as enjoyable as watching a beautifully coloured cockroach on your kitchen unit. And what's more, imagine the cockroach is trying to seduce you with lascivious touches.

'What is a terminator?' asked Grunt 1, still with his hands under his shirt.

'That's a machine,' Troglodyte started feeling horny, which made him bilious, 'a machine which is designed to terminate people.'

'Is that a cooking technique?' asked the hulk Grunt.

Troglodyte's eyes nearly popped out of their sockets. 'What?!'

'Oh... sorry... I thought it may have something to do with long-term food storage systems...'

'Oh my God! Were you humans before the esorcism?'

The suspicion in Grunt's mind increased. Troglodyte knew.

'To terminate means to kill.'

'Oh, I see,' Grunt tried to calm the situation but he wasn't too good at it. 'So why is it called a terminator? Why not just call it a killer?'

'Because... what a stupid question that is. I don't care why machines call it that. Even if they call it a garden fence it would still be an enemy.'

'All right, all right, sorry then. So tell me more about Connor. Seems the terminator hasn't succeeded, has he?'

'Sadly, he has. But he died together with Joe. Today, before esorcising you, we decided to esorcise him back.'

'What went wrong?'

'Everything went fine, but...'

'But?' Grunt asked and took his hands off his bosom at last for he had realized it would be absolutely useless in a man-to-man fight. And even a man-to-woman fight.

'The problem is we accidentally esorcised the terminator along with him.'

They watched the sad figure, struggling on the floor.

'Now he's trying to terminate himself.'

Troglodyte put a food bowl into the cage.

'Joe, food!' he called.

Connor crawled to the bowl, twitching as he moved. When he got there he buried his head into it. At that moment, the unguarded right hand rose up and hit the head from above, thus making it a part of the bowl.

'Let's go,' said Troglodyte to all three Grunts.

'Can't we do anything for him?' asked Grunt.

'Like what?'

'Like exorcise the terminator out.'

'Pardon me, young lady,[15] I hope you don't consider me a stupid exorcist?'

Then, he looked at Fat rat, standing on all fours next to the cage, sniffing the food bowl.

'Shouldn't we lock up your friend too?'

'Why? It's behaving naturally. It is a rat.'

'Rat? I thought it was a ferret.'

'No. Ferret is its name. But it's a rat.'

'You wanna tell me you've named a rat Ferret?'

'Well, not exactly. I called it Bamboo first.'

'Bamboo?'

'Well, yeah. But to the point, it is a Tro... I mean, a rat.'

'What did you want to say?'

'When?'

'Your tongue slipped. You said it is a Tro. I hope you didn't want to say Troglodyte?!' he said, menacingly.

'Great, that's what I really need right now,' Grunt thought, 'not only is he prepared to kill me because he

---

[15] There you can see how Troglodyte slowly adapts to the fact he is sexually attracted to a zombie and what is more, a zombie which considers herself a male.

knows I'm a machine but I've also offended him.' He thought hard how to resolve the situation.

'Of course I didn't,' he tried.

'What did you want to say then?'

'Ehm... well... a trolley-bus?' Grunt said the first 'Tro' word he could think of.

'A trolley-bus?'

'Yes, it's like a common bus but it is connected...'

'I know what a trolley-bus is!' Troglodyte interrupted him. 'I just don't understand how you could mistake a rat for a trolley-bus.'

'You know, Freud based most of his career on it. Embarrassing slips of the tongue. Like when you live alone with a herd of tiny sheep and you accidentally exchange the word runt for a c...'

'That's rubbish!' Troglodyte interrupted him to prevent the Author from using a swear word in the text. 'There is no similarity between a rat and a trolley-bus.'

'Of course there is. Take the shape, for example. The same aerodynamics.'

'Loads of things have the same shape.'

'Not a water pump, for instance.'

'It has when you lay it on its side,' Troglodyte countered.

'Are you telling me a rat and a water pump have the same shape?'

'No, I'm telling you a rat and a trolley-bus don't. Where do you have a tail, eh?'

'That's the trolley, of course.'

'Aren't there two trolleys?'

'Not necessary. The rat's eyes are similar to the trolley-bus lights. And they make similar noises."

'A trolley-bus creaks and hums.'

'And also whistles, as a rat does.'

'But a rat doesn't hum.'

'It could if it had gone through a difficult puberty.'

'A lot of things can make the same noises.'

'An example?'

Fortunately, Troglodyte's imagination was very poor so he decided to get a few sentences back in the dialogue: 'So, was it the rat we've eaten?'

'The same.'

'Did you possess it so it knocked herself out on our doorstep?'

'No, it did everything on its own will. It even led us to you.'

'Really? It's a shame we've eaten it, then. It must have been super intelligent. We could have sold it to a circus if we weren't so hungry.'

Grunt grimaced ironically: 'This one? To a sex-shop, maybe. When I remember how it tried to get into my tu...' he stopped, '...bby colon,' he finished awkwardly.

'Oh... lucky we were so hungry, then,' answered Troglodyte. Even with his poor imagination he felt uncomfortable in this case.

They left the hole and continued on their way through the tunnels. A few minutes later, they reached a dead end.

'That's it,' thought Grunt, 'we are trapped.' Curiously enough, Troglodyte didn't seem to be about to kill them.[16]

---

[16] You may think the author is too vague here because a human who thinks he may be killed in the next few minutes would be much more stressed. But he is not. A story character which has died so often during the story as Grunt has necessarily develops a certain immunity.

For instance, he was so lame he even walked in front of them. Grunt examined his back to see if it looked dangerous but didn't find anything threatening about human backs. Troglodyte had clearly made a fatal tactical error. Nevertheless, Grunt 1 and 2 slowed down to match his pace. Troglodyte reached the dead end. It seemed as its creators had died there from an unknown disease.[17] The tunnel ended suddenly and the floor was earthy, not stony as the rest of the tunnels were. Troglodyte took a shovel from the ground. Grunt had never seen anything like that. It looked dangerous.

'Don't lag behind, guys. Come here!'

Sure, thought Grunt. It's like a cat sitting in front of a mouse hole, saying: 'Come here!'

'Are we going or what?' asked Grunt.

'Oh, great, and a mouse would be so stupid it would come', he shook his head.

'Why?' he asked him.

'What? Why? I need you to dig with me.'

'I see.' This didn't persuade him at all. He didn't know what the word 'dicking' could mean but he knew it had some sexual connotation, 'And what is that thing?'

Troglodyte looked at the shovel as though he'd never seen it before.

'Do you mean the shovel?'

'Yes, yes. Deshovel. What is it for?'

'You dig with that, don't you?'

The situation immediately became clearer to Grunt. Troglodyte obviously thought these machines didn't understand human sexual behaviour. But Grunt worked in the right section to know all about that. You may dick a

---

[17] Lack of finance, probably.

sheep, you may dick a broken armchair, but there's no way to dick a shovel. Also, he couldn't believe anyone would lead him to a dead-end tunnel to have sex with a shovel.

'Fine, but I'll begin!' shouted Grunt from the distance.

'No problem,' shouted Troglodyte back. 'You can take a pickaxe. But I'm not sure that is the right work for a lady.'

'No, no, I want deshovel. And don't worry, she won't even touch it,' he pointed at his wife, now a huge beast which seemed to be able to carry a few tons of deshovels and massacre half of a town meanwhile.

'Okay,' Troglodyte shook his head, laid the shovel on the ground and crept off to find a new tool. Grunt approached the deshovel slowly. When he was halfway there he heard soft laughter. He reached the deshovel and realized the sound was coming from the ground at his feet.

'What's that?' he asked.

'That's why we are here,' answered Troglodyte. 'When we buried her we thought she was my old aunt. She was a good old undertakeress, oh yeah, the best one,' he looked dreamingly for a while, 'but she was one of them.'

'One of whom?'

'One of them, of course. The machines!' He lifted a tool, which made Grunt back away.

'What's wrong with you?' asked Troglodyte.

'What is that?'

'A pickaxe, of course.'

'Pickaxofource?'

'No, just pickaxe.'

'Juspickaxe?'

'Pickaxe!'

'Oh, I see. And what is it for?'

'For digging, of course.'

'As well? And shouldn't it be for pickaxing?'

'Call it for reading ladies' magazines if you want to.'

'What are you going to do with that?'

'Well... pickaxing, it seems.' He laughed. But right now, it seemed like the mad laughter of a maniac killer to Grunt. There was a buried machine, lying under their feet, and Troglodyte was looking forward to adding to his private graveyard.

'How do you pickaxe?'

'You know what? I will do that myself,' Troglodyte lost patience. 'Give me the shovel.'

'I won't!' shouted Grunt who considered deshovel to be his only chance for survival.

'We need to dig that machine out and throw it away. If you don't know how to dig, gimme the shovel!'

Grunt's head was buzzing. Dig the machine out? He may have missed something in the Section after all. He'd read about exhumations. And he knew how humans enjoyed dicking. Did it mean that all the time they sang songs about beautiful eyes and shining stars they were actually searching for someone to exhume with?

'Will you give me the shovel?!' Troglodyte started to sound very impatient.

'Only if you give me something in exchange.'

Troglodyte rolled his eyes. He had been thinking about a few more cages next to Connor's one for a while now.

'Okay, take a mattock then.' The tool he offered Grunt didn't look as strong as deshovel; it was much shorter and its melee attack was silly, compared with the other two tools. But still, there were three of them (he didn't count Riff-raff) and only one of Troglodyte. He couldn't use the deshovel and the pickaxe to attack them at the same time. That's why Grunt passed the deshovel to Troglodyte, grabbed the mattock and jumped back. Troglodyte shook his head and started digging.

It was soon clear there would be no fight. Troglodyte evidently didn't plan on pickaxing Grunt's head. Instead, he was uncovering the grave with the patience of an elementary school history teacher. The laughter became louder as each shovelful of earth was removed. Then at last, Troglodyte put the tools down. Grunt, still holding the mattock tightly, slowly moved forward and looked into the grave. There lay something which resembled a human corpse, but instead of rotting flesh, circuit elements poked through a bad skin imitation. There was no doubt, it was laughing loudly.

'A machine?' asked Grunt in amazement.

Troglodyte couldn't guess the real reason why Grunt was surprised. The existence of a machine didn't amaze him at all; the laughter did. After all, why couldn't humans bury a machine?

'Yep. A cootie.'

'A cootie?'

'A cootie.'

'What is a cootie?'

'I always forget how dumb you are. A cootie is a bug which lives in your hair unnoticed and sucks your blood.'

'I know what a cootie is!' said Grunt angrily, 'but I suppose you'd notice if this was living in your hair!'

'We call these cooties because they live in your family and you don't notice anything odd until they start laughing in the grave.'

'Why do they live in human families?'

'Spies. If it doesn't kill you itself it will call others that will.'

'How have you survived then?'

'A weird thing happens sometimes. The cootie may get involved with the people around and decide to stay with them.'

'Get involved? We are speaking about machines, aren't we?' A machine that likes people and laughs after death? Seems Grunt should have worked in a totally different section, like one which would gather information about machines.

'Weird, isn't it?'

'So your aunt really liked you?'

'My aunt as well as her successor.'

'Or it has killed you and you are a machine,' said Grunt.

'Yeah, or you,' laughed Troglodyte but he corrected himself then: 'No, you are not. We checked your body before the ritual.'

There was an awkward moment of silence. Grunt wanted to break it but he didn't know how.

'Can't you find out anyhow? I mean, while you're still alive.

'Well, you usually find out when your grandma tries to bite your head off. But I'm not sure if it meets the 'alive' requirement.'

Fat rat came to the grave in the meantime and examined its contents with interest.

'Why is it laughing?'

'Well, the scientists say it has something to do with disorganization of a biomass. But I think the machines just do that to show us how defenceless we are.'

'And why are you dicking it out?'

'We have to take it somewhere far from here so it doesn't interest the machines' sensors.'

'With the laughing?'

'Exactly. It can laugh as loud as it wants. But not in my graveyard!'

They came back to the den in which they lived. Troglodyte told them: 'There is a hole with a few straw mattresses, first on the right. It's empty. Sleep well. We'll go to the Rat hole tomorrow.'

Grunt shivered. A memory of what a rat might try to do next time he met one made some organs of his body contract. He hadn't had receptors in his tube before. It could be very unpleasant now.

'What is a rat hole?' he asked with a scared expression.

'Zion, of course,' Troglodyte looked at Grunt's expression and started to laugh. 'Don't be afraid. We only call it a rat hole. There are no rats in Zion.'

Grunt heaved a sigh of relief.

'They've all been killed by the brown rats,' finished Troglodyte.

Grunt had to process this information before asking: 'Troglodyte?'

'Hm?'

'What is a brown rat?'

'It's a much bigger rat.'

Grunt absolutely failed to notice the malice with which the information was imparted.

'A bigger one?'

'Yes.'

'A lot bigger?'

'Yes.'

'How much?'

Troglodyte extended his arms to indicate a size which could easily refer to a bear.

'You can't imagine how happy I am to hear that.'

Troglodyte watched Grunt with suspicion. 'You're weird,' he stated the obvious.

Suddenly, Grunt had an idea.

'I wonder, Troglodyte... Can I ask you something about the cooties?'

'Fire away.'

'Do I need to?'

'I thought you wanted to.'

'Which way?'

'What?'

'Which way should I fire?'

'Why would you fire at anything?'

They stared at each other in amazement.

'You told me to fire away. So I wanted to know...'

'Oh,' Troglodyte understood at last. 'It's just an expression. It means "tell me".'

'It does?'

'Yeah.'

'The section would pay a fortune for such information,' Grunt let slip.

'What?'

Grunt tried to look confused: 'What?'

'What did you say?'

'When?'

'Now.'

'Now?'

'Yes.'

'What?'

'That's what I wanna know.'

'And what is that?' Grunt thought he could extricate himself from the problem.

'That thing you've just said.'

'Just now?'

'Yes.'

'I think I said: "And what is that?"''

'I mean before that.'

'Oh, before that!' Grunt laughed as if he had just understood.

'Exactly,' said Troglodyte happily. They seemed to be getting somewhere.

'If I'm not mistaken,' said Grunt, 'I said: "what?"''

Troglodyte's smile faded. 'Not that! Before that!'

'I'm not sure. I think I said another "what" before the last "what"'.

Troglodyte decided to use a straight question: 'Did you say anything about a section of some kind?'

'What?'

'What what?'

'Well... what?'

Troglodyte started to get upset: 'What "what"? What the hell do you mean?'

'What?' asked Grunt, now truly confused.

'I asked you if you said anything about any section. Did you?'

'No. But I definitely said some more "whats"'.

'You know what?'

'What?'

'Go to hell with that "what" of yours.'

'Hell?'

'Yeah!'

'Where is it?'

Troglodyte was becoming red in the face: 'Would you tell me what it was you wanted to ask me?'

'What?'

'Say "what" one more time and I'll do something so nasty you'll not forget it till the end of the day.'

'What?'

'I'm warning you, Grunt!'

'Well... it doesn't seem to be so bad, does it? I mean, if I remember it only till the end of the day...'

'Incidentally, the end of the day will be also the end of your life,' growled Troglodyte.

'Oh, I see.'

'So tell me what you wanted to ask about those machines.'

'Oh, sure. I wanted to ask you if there has ever been any documented case of these cooties really calling any reinforcements.'

Troglodyte was so pleased he had finally been asked a straight and understandable question that he tried to think about the answer more carefully than usual. 'I'm not sure. A friend of mine had one in his family but that was the same case as with my aunt. And I knew a guy whose brother gave him a land mine as a Christmas present. The answer to your question is, no, I don't know about any specific case of cooties calling in reinforcements. But everyone knows they do that.'

'Forget what everyone knows. Has there ever been any reported case of cooties calling reinforcements?'

Troglodyte was impressed. The stupid debate might have a useful outcome after all. 'Now I think about it, no, there hasn't. That's crazy, Grunt. What does it mean?'

'What?'

'Don't you ever say "what" again in front of me! Why did you ask me that?'

'Well, I wanted to know the answer.'

'Of course you wanted to know the answer, you idiot! That's the whole point of questioning, isn't it?'

'Exactly my point.'

'But you wanted to know the answer for some reason.'

'I didn't.'

Troglodyte got seriously angry. 'You didn't?!' he shouted. 'Are you telling me you asked that just for the sake of it?'

'Sure.'

'So you haven't discovered anything new about the cooties?'

'No, I haven't.'

'I hate you, Grunt. I really do!' and he stormed away.

Grunt left their hole the following morning, surprised by the events of the previous night - because there had been none. He had wanted to examine the possibilities of the human body with Grunt. Instead, it seemed like it was only minutes after they lay down on something which could not be called straw mattresses even in Brazilian slums that they were awaken by Troglodyte again. Since it really was morning, Grunt realized he hadn't been aware of anything that had happened during the whole night. His hulk wife had an even bigger problem. She'd never heard anything about sleeping, yawning or horribly lame legs.

Troglodyte led them to something that he called a 'kitchen' but which actually resembled a bombed toilet u-bend. Troglodyte and two other people sat there.[18]

'This is Donna,' said Troglodyte. Donna waved happily. 'And this is Gravefiller. Well... to be honest, we are all sort of grave fillers. And sometimes diggers.' He was waiting for an unsatisfied reaction which didn't come. 'But Gravefiller is a gravedigger who really loves filling graves.'

'Yeah!' said Gravefiller. 'Let's bury some rats!'

'But Troglodyte,' asked Grunt, 'didn't you say there are no rats in Zion? That they have all been driven out by bears?'

'Brown rats.'

'Sure, brown rats.'

'Black or white, slam on sight' sang Gravefiller happily.

'We will bury people, of course,' Troglodyte explained. 'We just call them rats.'

'Oh, I see, a metonymy.' Grunt understood.

'Exactly!' Donna was excited. 'It is a sort of extrapolation. A transition of meaning from one subject to another.'

Troglodyte ignored her absolutely. 'We may not find any rats, Gravefiller,' he answered Gravefiller instead. 'You know how hard it is.'

'So I'll slam them with a shovel and *then* we'll find them.'

The hulk Grunt entered the debate: 'But Troglodyte, why do we dig corpses in? I thought we searched for food. Shouldn't we dig them out instead?'

Fortunately, Troglodyte didn't understand what Grunt had meant. 'We will bury the corpses, then charge their families to get some credits. These we use for buying the

---

[18] At least one of them could have been mistaken for a human.

food. We do have some replicators but those beasts are broken most of the time. And even if they *do* work I sometimes feel like the replicator would be tastier than the food it makes.'

'But why don't we just eat the...'

'Tell me more about that community thing,' Grunt interrupted her loudly so the word '...corpses' was obscured by the sound of his voice, 'Are there more such communities?'

Troglodyte knew that this would come. It always did. Most people didn't want to spend their lives as undertakers. 'There are,' he answered reluctantly.

'Many?'

'Hm.'

'Is the whole society divided into communities?'

'Yep.'

'And Troglodyte...' Troglodyte knew what was coming. Grunt would show interest in other communities and they would all leave, 'is it called communism?' finished Grunt, who'd read something about the People's Republic of China while working in the Section.

Troglodyte wasn't able to answer. Donna, on the other hand, was: 'Not exactly. In communism, the whole society is one community.'

'So, what is this called?'

'Dunno. What about a "controlled anarchy"?'

'Are we going to make the corpses, or what?' said Gravefiller, trying to return to the main topic.

'And who will we force to pay for the corpses we buy?' asked the hulk Grunt, still unsure about the mechanics of trading; at least, the mechanics of this type of trading, anyway.

'Anyone,' answered Troglodyte.

'And why don't they just... throw them away.' She understood from her husband's previous reaction that the sentence shouldn't be: 'Why don't they just eat them.'

'They would certainly like to. That's why we need to search the city to catch them red-handed and force them to pay for a decent burial.'

'Force them? How?'

'Easy. Gravefiller will just tell them...'

'Gimme money or I'll slam you,' finished Gravefiller, holding a shovel in his hand.

'Are you blackmailing them?'

'It is an old tradition. Undertaking has always been a blackmailing profession. How else can you get people to pay a fortune for something so worthless? Have you heard about the pyramids? Those guys knew how to make money.'

'Got it!' shouted Grunt happily, after few minutes of a silent debate with Donna. 'So communism means they are all one happy, not-working community. Anarchy means there are communities inside a no-community society. Am I right?[19]'

Gravefiller squinted at Donna and Grunt with disgust.

'I have an idea,' he said to Troglodyte.

'What idea?' asked Troglodyte.

'Let's bury them.'

While Gravefiller was happily singing a mournful song about an orphan child which desperately wanted to join its mother in the grave, the group reached a pretty

---

[19] No, he wasn't. In fact it's much worse.

luxurious looking hole, with a big sign over the doorway: 'Delicate Goodies, Delicate prizes'. There was definitely someone really rich living here, clearly running a business in the food industry.[20] Troglodyte hammered on the door. A window opened somewhere on one of the higher floors and then, obviously when this building inhabitant had found out who was at the door, the window closed very, very silently.

'I know you are home,' shouted Troglodyte. 'In the name of a dignified death, open the door!'

Even if a north wind blew throughout the house not a curtain would move now.

'The Grave committee is here,' Troglodyte continued calmly. 'Open the door or we will break it down! We know you are hiding a corpse!'

The inhabitant of the house clearly thought it better to deal with the situation face to face[21] because footsteps sounded from behind the door. A part of a face appeared in the door's eye-hole. Gravefiller prepared the shovel handle for the possibility he'd need to insert it in this eye-hole.

'Good morning,' said the man, although it was clear that the morning he really wished the gravediggers included a red sky, rivers of blood, and a black figure, expanding its wings over the horizon. 'I'm sorry, I didn't hear you. I must have fallen asleep.'

He didn't know that he could expect to experience that sweet, delightful feeling again soon. Without the necessity of waking up.

---

[20] A white meat, probably.

[21] Since he saw the visitors with his own eyes he was obviously suffering a nasty mental disease of some kind.

'Give us the corpse and pay!' ordered Troglodyte.

'But there is no corpse in here,' answered the man. 'Who told you that nonsense?'

'We have our sources.'

'Someone made fools of you.'

Gravefiller approached the eye-hole, looking dangerous.

'But there is something else for you,' said the man quickly.

'What?' asked Troglodyte.

'Well, you gravediggers are really hard guys and...' he winked at Grunt 1 and 2, 'hot ladies...'

'So?'

'I have a job for you.'

'We don't work. We fill graves!'

'Wait, Murderer,[22]' Troglodyte stopped Gravefiller, 'What would that be?'

'It is nice easy work...'

'I may let you enjoy yourself, Murderer...'

'For 30 credits per day.'

The Grave council members looked at each other. Thirty credits was enough to buy a well-baked rat on Zion main street- if only all the rats hadn't been driven out by brown rats.

'So what does the job involve?'

---

[22] People who don't know the syndicates' background usually think its members are generally called Kerny the Crusher, Tonny the Killer or Robert the Cleaner. It may be really inconvenient to let the public* know their real names, as Will Bamber, Ted Piggie or Willie Dungworth.

* Those who are located on the less favourable side of a gun**.

** It's the one usually equipped with a silencer.

'I breed a few cute little animals and I don't have enough time to look after them. So, you'd just need to feed them, and perhaps play with them a little.

'What animals?'

'They can even speak a little.'

'Parrots?' asked Donna with hope in her voice.

'No, not exactly...'

'So...' Donna went white, 'are they Krossins?'

'Dear lady, only a madman would breed Krossins.'

'You don't know how happy I am to hear you say that.'

'Great. Because, in fact, they are Krossins.'

'But you just said...'

'Yes, I must be a madman. What sane person would pay 30 credits a day?'

'What sane person would take such an offer?'

'Wait, Donna,' Troglodyte interrupted her, 'We really need that money.'

'But no one...'

'On the contrary,' Troglodyte turned to the three Grunts, 'this is when your community needs you.'

Grunt, Grunt, Grunt and Fat rat went to a room where a few hairy spheres ran here and there. The cage floor was covered in bones, blood, feathers and many more things in various stages of nibblation. When the group came in the Krossins stopped their activities (nibbling anything in the cage that remained to be nibbled on). Two of them bit the cage wire while the other two sat facing them, showing their teeth, which were a little too big, compared to their bodies.

'Aren't they cute?' said the owner, with tenderness in his voice, as if these were cute puppies. 'And they can even

talk. A big speaker is Tuffy here but he seems to be busy.'
He pointed towards a sphere which was gnawing the
fencing. 'But little Furryball here is good too, aren't you,
Furball?'

'Snuffff!' growled Furryball towards them.

'See? I told you they are sweet. You'll have lot of fun. See
you,' and he left the room so quickly a bullet train would
envy him.

'It's weird,' said hulk Grunt while they watched a
herd of monsters trying to demolish the cage, 'that he
never told us when he is coming back. This can't hold
long,' she pointed at the hardly resisting fencing and the
hungry expressions on the Krossins' evil faces.

'He may be right, they could be fine,' tried Grunt 1,
clinging to hope. He summoned his courage and
approached the cage. But he changed his mind a few
seconds after that because the Furryball burst out in evil
laughter, which made Grunt jump back. Tuffy let go of
the fencing for a while and sang in a rough voice: 'Yer
dead, ye deadie dead,' which Furryball accompanied by a
vile growling. Another Krossin looked straight at Grunt
and said: 'Me go down on ye like no one beforrrr!'

'I wonder,' said Grunt in a low voice, 'why Troglodyte
sent us. If these holy creatures walk with someone it
would definitely be Gravefiller.'

After a half an hour, it was clear that although the
cage was made from a durable material it couldn't
survive the Krossins' attacks. It was badly damaged in
many places and the Krossins didn't seem inclined to give
it a rest.

'We should definitely do something,' said Grunt 2,
expressing the obvious.

'Run?' proposed Grunt - an obvious solution for an obvious truth.

They stormed towards the door. Grunt just wrenched the handle off.

'That son of a bitch!'

Grunt 1 and 2 struggled to break the door down but both his delicate bodies managed only to get some bruises.

'I'll try,' said hulk Grunt.

'Why?' asked Grunt 1 and 2.

'So we can get out.'

'Why do you think you can burst through when I couldn't?'

'Because I'm bigger and stronger.'

'You certainly are not!' Grunt refused to accept the obvious truth. He had a slight problem with his new gender.

Grunt just pushed him aside and stormed the door. But her efforts ended with the same results as before. Despite the tough situation, it pleased her husband.

'It's all right,' he said, 'when the Krossins get out of the cage they'll bite through the door.'

'Grunt?'

'Hm?'

'Don't you think there's something missing from your calculations?'

'What?'

'Us.'

The Krossins' efforts were very effective. Now all four monsters were widening out one of the holes they'd made. Although they sometimes bit each other by mistake (or at least it seemed like a mistake) they were continuing at a terrifying speed.

'Maybe,' said Grunt 1, 'there is a way to calm them.'

'How?' asked him Grunt.

'Like babies.'

'Do you know what human mothers do when their children are trying to eat them?'

'Well, I've read a story like that. It was called 'Little Otik'. A story of a couple whose child had an insatiable appetite. It tried to eat its parents too.'

'And what did they do?'

'They didn't do anything. It ate them.'

Grunt watched him in disbelief. 'Great. I'm much calmer now.'

'But we could sing to them.'

'Why?'

'That's what human mothers do when their children won't calm down.'

'Did anyone sing to Little Otik?'

'I think no one had time for that.'

'All right, try. We have few minutes before they go down on us like no one has before.'

Grunt was thinking frantically but nothing crossed his mind.

'It must be because of the heart beat,' he thought. 'If I was a machine I'd just search the database and... and I won't sing anything because machines can't sing.'

Suddenly, she sang shakily: 'Sma-ll child became orphan...'

Sure, Gravefiller's hit number one! How could he have forgotten that? He joined Grunt: 'Small child became orphan, because of a lame gun, because of a lame gun.'

The Krossins stopped in their efforts. The Grunts had gained their attention.

'When it became older, saw the mother's boulder...'

The Krossins, one by one, started laughing frantically. The voice sounded as if something small, leathery and very unfortunate had come too close to a grass-cutter. It wasn't an expected reaction. It was still a good one though for the Krossins stopped demolishing the cage at last.

'She lies in the graveyard, at least some of her parts...'

It was definitely working.

'Oh mother my dearest, speak a bit to me, please,
I cannot, my child, there is mud in my mouth...'

It was a very long and sad song. Nevertheless, it ended ten minutes later with the words:

'It died, it died. Oh God, the child died.'

The Krossins were rolling on the floor for a while but when they realized the song had ended entirely they directed their evil stares at their new caretakers again.

'Anything else, quick!'

Now, Grunt remembered the Elvis' hit 'Love me tender' which was so romantic it would make even Keira Knightley puke, so it definitely wasn't the right song for Krossins. But with a few small alterations...

'Knock my legs off,
Knock my feet,
Never let me go,
Just please, Darling, give me head,
Your brain is juicy so.'

It was good. Another leathery creature ended in a grass-cutter.

'Shoot my hands off,

Shoot my feet,
Just not my zombie mouth,
Just, my Darling, give me head,
Let's zombie with me.'
He repeated the last verse and finished.
'Very nice, but a little too short,' said his wife.
But this was what Grunt always dreamed of. Their survival was based on his ability to improvise. So he actually had to create crazy things and all the others (Grunt and Krossins) had to listen.
He remembered another song, 'Scarborough Fair'. He didn't have to think too long...
'Are you lying in Scarborough grave,' he laughed himself. That was really absurd.
'Flies and worms and field mice and moles,
Remember me to one who lies there,
The horny corpse who hired me as a whore.
Tell him he left something in me there,
Horny corpse and big decayed hole,
I'd like to know who sent it and where,
Until it was eaten by a mole.'
The Krossins were laughing like mad spheres and it seemed Furryball was playing the horny corpse. He tried to invite Tuffy to be his co-actor and give him the role of the other corpse, which resulted in a short fight between them. Grunt was thinking how to change a 'cambric shirt'. But he soon had a solution:
'Tell him to give back my carpal bone,'
Flies and worms and field mice and moles,
That fetishist scum have stolen my bone,
While I was searching for my pelvis bone.'

And thus it continued for a few more hours. They went through 'What shall we do with a leaking sailor', with Furryball playing a leaking sailor, a film song 'Dirty dying: End of my life' where Furryball played John Travolta, 'The Twelve Dead at Christmas,' where the Krossins had a real problem with impersonating Christmas. And then, while singing 'Four Dead Whores', (I'd rather not describe what the Krossins were doing during that), the owner arrived at last. In fact, before he came in, a gas which paralyzed the Krossins had been released into the room. It was clearly some sort of anti-Krossin substance which the owner had somehow forgotten to mention. It smelled like lilies of the valley. The owner entered soon after that. When he saw his new caretakers complete with all their limbs and definitely very alive, he froze in amazement. Then he tried to run away but hulk Grunt was faster. She seized him by his neck and lifted him off the ground. She was positively surprised at how easy it was.

'So you wanted to use us as a Yummy-Krossin?' she asked dangerously.

'Yum... what?'

'As Krossin food?'

'What?' asked the owner and Grunt 1 at the same time. But only Grunt was really surprised.

'How would you like being hit with a shovel?'

'Not... not much,' the owner croaked through his compressed throat. Grunt looked at his wife with horror. She had never been so vile. Was it possible his singing had put her into such a mood?

'Let's trade,' Grunt continued while still holding the owner by his throat, 'Give us three hundred credits. As a reward, we won't lock you in. That's fair, isn't it?'

'I don't have...' he tried. She raised her fist dangerously.

When Grunt, Grunt, Grunt and Fat rat had come back to the Grave-diggers' den Donna came running to great them.

'You're back! That's awesome! That's unbelievable. I told Troglodyte off for what he did. I told him he's an egoistic and egocentric person with a Nietzsche-Machiavellian fascistic discourses which mistakes the temporary possession of borrowed will for an absolutist monarchy which clashes with tyranny dangerously.'

'Did you really say that to him?' Grunt 2 asked in awe.

'I did,' Donna seemed to be proud of herself.

'And what did he say?'

'Well,' Donna immediately seemed less confident, 'he looked at me for a while and then he said: 'What?''

'Oh, a good old What,' smiled Grunt, 'and what did you do then?'

'I repeated it.'

'And then?'

'Then... well... he left. But it doesn't matter. How did you kill them?'

'Who?'

'The Krossins, of course!'

'Were we expected to kill them?!

'No, not necessary... especially if you didn't want to stay alive... how did you stay alive then?'

'We sang to them.'

Donna looked from one to the other, waiting for an outburst of suppressed laughing. It didn't come.

'You really mean that?'

'Sure.'

Donna shook her head and sighed: 'If only my aunt knew that... So, how much did you get?'

'My dear wife played Robocop, so three hundred.'

'You're kidding!' Donna was positively fascinated. 'Three hundred? Three? I mean... wow! There will surely be a big feast. We may even open a bottle of that pure water from the twenty-first century. If Troglodyte hasn't purloined that already. And Frenzer may show us some of his wheelchair tricks... well... if Troglodyte hasn't purloined his wheelchair too.'

The return of the survivors meant a great commotion, which was followed by great merriment when the community found out the money they had made. According to Troglodyte, it wasn't enough to open the pure-water bottle (which, Grunt thought, probably meant Troglodyte had really purloined that) but a great feast followed nevertheless. A feast where there was food present which was in a real form, sometimes even with colours and what was more, it was made from something of a biological origin. In any case, it was much better than most of the usual food found in school canteens of the twentieth century.

Even Joe Connor was there, obviously trying not to hurt himself. When he saw Grunt he went up to him.

'Hey, Joe,' Grunt tried a non-committal conversation. But as he said 'Joe', Joe took advantage of his open mouth and put a toffee in it. Then, he shouted: 'You're terminated!' turned around and went off.

Grunt chewed the toffee and wondered what its former owner wanted to tell him. The toffee wasn't bad. It was something between plastic and... well... plastic. Okay, it tasted like common plasticine but it was as good as most of the food Grunt had tried during his short human life. After all, elementary school children take pleasure in eating all available variations of chalk, glue or blackboards even though they will get a fairly adequate meal in the school canteen soon after that.

While he was chewing the toffee, Troglodyte came up to him and started speaking with a pompous voice and gestures: 'Welcome to our feast. You are our guests of honour today. You can take the seats of honour which are usually reserved for myself.' He pointed at four round metal pieces of junk next to the table. Fat rat ran towards one of them, attacked it and rolled sideways with it.

'As the elected member and representative of the Gravedigger committee I'd like to pronounce you, with the agreement with the community policy...' he paused.

'What are you chewing?'

'Joe gave it to me,' answered Grunt.

'Again?' said Troglodyte wearily. 'Just spit it out,' he returned to the official tone. 'So, as I said, in the name of the Gravedigger committee whose elected member...'

'Why?'

'What?'

'Why should I spit it out?'

'Because it is plastic explosive. So where was I? Oh yes... in the name of...'

'Why did he give me plastic explosive?'

'His two personas seem to have reached some sort of agreement. So he tries to terminate as many others as he can but also as ineffectively as he can. Oh yes, and tell him you have spat it out or he will follow you with his 'My-first-blast' kit everywhere you go, trying to attach wires to your belly.'

Grunt spat out the toffee and called to Joe: 'Hey, Joe, I've spat out the toffee.'

'So, as I said before, I'd like to officially...'

'It wasn't a toffee,' called Joe back, 'it was plastic explosive.'

'I see,' answered Grunt.

'...of course, by the name of the Gravedigger...'

'No worries. I'll give you another one.'

'What now?' asked Grunt.

'...committee whose elected member... what?'

'What should I do now?'

'I don't know. Tell him you don't want any.'

'I don't want any,' shouted Grunt.

'...the Gravedigger committee whose...'

'Positive?'

'Positive.'

'... elected member and castrative I am...'

'You are sly. Don't you wanna be a terminator?'

'What now?'

Troglodyte gave up at last: 'Tell him you don't.'

'I don't.'

'Pity,' answered Joe and went to the feasting crowd to see if he could find anyone keen to let him terminate them.

'He is much better, isn't he?' said Grunt.

'Yeah,' answered Troglodyte, 'much more conscious.'

'How long has he been behaving like that?'

'It was about eight o'clock when he actually stopped beating himself and started asking people if they wouldn't mind being terminated.

'What did they answer?'

'He was unlucky. The first one he met was Donna. She started explaining something about...' he paused to find the exact expression in his memory, 'moral aspects of activities intended to cross-platform on behalf of another person... Anyway, she was the first one he tried to terminate.'

'With a toffee?'

'With a fireman's axe.'

When the feast ended (after about a quarter of an hour of discreet but all the more vicious fighting for any consumable food[23]) the members of the Grave

---

[23] Did you ever wonder why mothers teach their children not to put their elbows on the table? Their usual argument that only savage natives eat like that isn't entirely wrong, but also isn't entirely right. The thing is, the less food is on the table the more elbow-work is needed to get it. The extraordinary evolution of European civilization started by the poorer classes trying to mimic the richer ones and all their manners, hoping that someone might mistake them in the future and give them some free money. Since the manners included the absence of elbows on the table the poorer classes had to start using their heads when fighting for the food. This soon resulted in the poor people being much cleverer than the nobility, and thus the basics for democratic society were established.

When the food crisis struck Europe during the First World War most of the people returned to their basic instincts of using the elbows intead of the head for fighting. The only nation which still kept to the right habits was Germany, which is why the Prussian

Committee had their time for suggesting what to do with the money the Grunts had brought in.

'So, we're agreed.' Troglodyte summarized the previous boring debate which I want to spare you from. 'Half of the money will be spent on food. But we can have some luxury goods. What would you like to buy?'

'Clothes,' said someone.

'Boots,' suggested another.

'Why boots? Gloves!' said Frenzer.

'Shovels with blade-equipped handles!' said Gravefiller dreamily.

'Library,' tried Donna. Everyone looked at her with disgust. A very thin man stood up and said: 'I'm going to hang myself.'

'Don't be stupid, Skeleton,' Troglodyte called back to him. 'Sit down and vote. Hang yourself after the polls are closed. So, Donna's suggestion has been rejected.'

'Hey!' Donna looked hurt.

'The other ones will be put to a vote. Any other ideas?'

'What about an advertisement?' said Grunt.

'Sure!' Donna was excited. She was obviously used to having her ideas rejected so she wasn't too disappointed her new library had been rejected as well. 'That's a great idea. An addition to the undertaker services. I can see the slogans: "Your dead are watching you; give them a proper burial". Or for those who have thrown their loved ones away and now their conscience bothers them: "Give your dead the best death day possible."'

The community members didn't seem too sure about this idea. Grunt knew immediately that if his suggestion was going to be successful he needed to say he didn't agree

---

helmet was equipped with a spike on its top.

with Donna at all. The problem was he'd meant exactly what Donna said.

'I meant something a little different,' Grunt tried to gain some time.

'How?' asked Troglodyte. 'Some time' had already gone.

'I won't do an ad for undertaking services but for dying itself. Like: "Say NO to life" or "Having a headache? Die."'

'But that's complete lunacy,' answered Donna. 'This won't persuade anyone to do anything.'

The reaction was exactly as Grunt expected: 'Why not?' said Skeleton. 'It would definitely persuade me.'

'Yeah, but you commit suicide every other day.'

'Because of you, egghead. You're the best ad for death I've ever known.'

Troglodyte entered the debate: 'I think the idea isn't bad at all.'

'Of course it is,' answered Donna, grumpily. But the more she was against it the more the others were for it.

'We could emphasise life conditions,' added Gravefiller, 'like: "Tired of eating replicated shit? Die."'

'And I'd go even farther than that,' added Skeleton. "It can't be worse than it is now. So what are you waiting for?"

'But that's total nonsense.'

It was clear to all this was nonsense. But the fact Donna hated it so much gave it an extra sweet taste.

'I think it's brilliant,' continued Troglodyte. 'We'll spam the city with leaflets saying "Does your life have any sense?" That may bring someone to us. And we could spread slogans such as: "Suicide is a proud death!" And we'll create a registry of proud death where those who wish to commit suicide would enter their names so any inhabitant of Zion could find them there and see how proud they were. That way, we won't lose them.'

'And if it doesn't work we'll just display Donna's face,' added Skeleton. Donna grimaced, offended.

'Right then,' said Troglodyte, though it wasn't clear if he was continuing with his speech or reacting to the Skeleton's comment. 'Who votes for an advertisement?'

It seemed at last that Grunt's plan was successful. Sure, he hadn't meant a registry of proud death and he wasn't sure this would work. But it was an ad nevertheless. And even if he had wanted to step back, all hands except those of Donna and Ferret were in the air.

'Let's get some paper then.'

Even though there was nothing on the table which bore any resemblance to food (the only things which didn't look like pieces of burnt, urinated upon and fossilized troglodytes were Joe's plastic explosives) the community members still didn't want to end the feast and return to their common lives which were even worse than the feast. Gravefiller brought some fungi that he claimed were magic mushrooms. Since no one knew in what way they were magical nobody touched them before the dealer did. Grunt was sitting next to Donna and was speaking with her to make up to her for his dirty trick during the voting.

'I see,' said Grunt. 'So you've all been in that thing? The matrix?'

'Sure,' Donna answered. 'In the illusion world, created by machines. How come you don't remember that?'

'I... well... lost my memory during the esorcism.'

'I see.'

Grunt was trying to remember if he'd heard anything about the matrix in the Section. He couldn't think of anything although that didn't mean he hadn't actually heard about it. The human memory was so chaotic he couldn't even be sure he hadn't been looking at the matrix report five minutes ago. Still, this was weird...

'Are you sure about the machines?'

'Sure.'

'How come?'

'I'm not sure what are you asking, Grunt.'

'How can you be sure machines are responsible?'

'Well...' Donna looked uncertain. 'It makes sense, doesn't it? The machines need energy from human emotions.'

'What do they need?' asked Grunt, positively amazed.

'The energy of human emotions.'

'Why?'

'Because they can't get it from the sun.'

Grunt recapitulated all the types of fuel he and the other machines around him needed to run their bodies. He wasn't able to find any possible use of the energy from sun. And he knew what the sun was. People were babbling about it all the time. 'The sunset is beautiful, isn't it?' 'You're the sun of my life,' 'Let's kill our sun'. All the time. It was nonsense. Absurd. Imagine a machine, let's say a sludge pump which one day finds out it can't use the energy from the sun. Therefore, to compensate for this depressing handicap, it enslaves a human to use its emotions instead. And even if Grunt had been able to give the right of existence to the scheme of a grass-cutter, happily bathing in the waves of human emotions, he still couldn't avoid one ultimate question.

'How?' he asked.

'How what?'

'How do they use the energy of human emotions?'

'When humans feel emotions the electric voltage in their bodies changes.'

This was even more absurd. If you run a common bicycle dynamo you'd have more energy than from thousands of people connected to an alternating current field. You couldn't get enough energy from a year of emotions of a human trapped in the middle of a war even to run one tentacle for an hour. If the machines used all the energy they spent on keeping the connected humans alive and applied it to rubbing ebonite sticks with fox tails, their work would be much more effective.

But then, Donna started speaking about Kant's imperatives and Grunt lost his train of thought.

The next day, Grunt 1 and 2 woke up, left Grunt sleeping (and, as a male body should, snoring like an elephant) and went out of the hole to make the always broken replicator create a mass which could reach the stomach before the body realized what had happened and returned it. When Grunt entered the kitchen he met Donna, who was obviously trying to do the same.

'No sense in trying,' said Donna hungrily. 'Doesn't work, as usual.'

'Oh,' said Grunt, disappointed.

'How did you like our debate yesterday?'

Grunt was surprised she referred to her monologue as a 'debate'. He certainly hadn't enjoyed it much but he didn't want to hurt her feelings.

'Is it possible that a simple yes or no is expected from me?'

He had said the right thing because Donna's reaction was positive: 'Sure, you are a philosopher through and through, aren't you?'

'Is it expected from me again?'

'I thought that maybe...' Donna seemed to be shy for some reason, 'maybe we could go together...'

Grunt had read something about that. Going out with Donna? Well...

'...to the church.'

Grunt was confused again.

'Since you've got such a philosophical soul, I thought you might like to see the election of the new Pope. It will be a great event. The day after tomorrow.'

Before Grunt could answer, Troglodyte came into the room.

'Hey, Grunt! Alive at last. Come with me. I need to show you our doorway.'

'You're so tactless, Troglodyte,' said Donna. 'We were having a nice talk.'

'This is much more important than your rambling about the meaning of the universe.'

'Only because you can't advance beyond your pitiful existence!'

This was the most unpleasant thing Donna had said to anyone during the time he'd known her. Troglodyte should say something really strong and intelligent to crush her.

'You're a bitch,' said Troglodyte. 'Come on, Grunt, follow me,' and he went out of the room. Grunt looked at Donna apologetically and followed him.

'Tell me when you come back. So we can arrange it,' she shouted after him.

'And Troglodyte,' said Grunt when they had left Donna so far behind she wouldn't overhear them and thus realize how unable he had been to advance beyond his own pitiful existence, 'could I have something to eat, first?'

After they had eaten a roughly cooked brown rat's wing Troglodyte said: 'Right. So, now to the doorway.'

'I thought I knew the way out. We've been there, remember?'

'We sneaked out by the back door. It's absolutely secret. That's why it takes so long to get to Zion - because we must go a much longer way around. But I may assign you to a listening post at the doorway for some time so you should know where it is.'

'So what is the doorway?'

'The main entrance. It is our official address.'

'And the listening post?'

'Come, I'll show you.'

They came to a big open door behind which a Zion street could be seen. There was a metallic doormat in the middle of the doorway. On the wall, opposite the doorway, a banner hung: 'Do you want to die? We will arrange all the necessary steps. More information inside.'

Troglodyte pointed at it. 'Good, isn't it? I made it myself this morning.'

'Nice,' said Grunt, 'only the drawing below is lame. I suppose it is Donna?'

'Yeah,' smiled Troglodyte. 'Good, isn't it?'

Suddenly, a man came round the corner. This was clearly a member of the Grave committee that Grunt had not met. His personal story is not important so I won't bore you with it. Let's say he had chosen a permanent listening post duty after Troglodyte's desperate pleading of the 'do this or die' type. If he dies a really interesting and funny death during the story I will inform you. For now, let's call him William the Listener.

'So,' Troglodyte said, 'this is the most direct way to Zion. The problem is that it's watched, so we can't go through it.'

'Watched? By whom?'

'By the City council. Always when we go to Zion through this doorway the City council sends notices to all prominent people of the city, and then they are all immediately alive and kicking. You won't believe what some of them can do. There was even a boy, some Kevin, who actually tried to fool us by pulling his dead parents around with ropes behind the window.'

'All right, then. And what about the listening post duties?'

'Sometimes, someone comes to visit us. Mostly to collect taxes, or to kill us, or well... for all the not very nice reasons you can imagine. When someone from the Committee comes in he walks around the doormat. So we know he is one of us.' He watched Grunt's confused expression. Then, he stamped on the doormat. A voice like a litter disposer crushing a proper Soviet armour vehicle sounded. Grunt understood: 'Sure. So if any intruder comes they stamp on the doormat and the person on listening post duty knows we need to be careful.'

'Exactly. We used to put land mines there but one day Frenzer went home tanked up and he forgot.'

'Dear Lord! So that's how he...'

'It blasted his wheelchair off.'

'Oh.'

'We spent three months hunting for parts to create a new one. So we decided to change the strategy and use the doormat instead."

Donna did as she'd promised and took him to the election of the new Zion Pope. He went only with one body so he could do something more interesting in the other one if the election was too dull. He tried to... well... communicate with Grunt with his second body but she, for some reason, ignored him.

Grunt and Donna went unnoticed by the night Zion[24] and came to a white hole whose wall was covered by a big banner: 'House of the Dog' which, Grunt thought, was obviously a misspelling of 'House of the God.' He was mistaken though. This was in fact just a fragment of a bigger banner which had said:

'House of the Dog

By Him shall be broken,

Bitches and cubs

By Hell fire be taken,

Only the pure ones

---

[24] All right, sure there wasn't anything like a night since Zion was completely located underground. I just wanted you to imagine the feeling of a romantic night town. The street-lamps, casting their dim light on abandoned pavements. Abandoned horses, casting shadows on the dimly lit pavements. And tons of abandoned horse excrement you splash into because you don't see nothing in the fucking dim lights and the crappy shadows. And of course the unforgettable street gangs preparing for a night of merry-making, accompanied by an orchestra of death rattling. Simply the best time for a romantic date.

Will be awoken.'

The rest of the banner had been stolen by the Grave committee members soon after it had been put up. The undertakers used it for filling caskets for priests so they had something to read when they awoke.

They went into a big chamber. In the middle, two rows of strange characters wearing violet tabards and furious expressions sat opposite one another. The head of the table was occupied by a man, sitting on a big throne made of shiny oil barrels. He was wearing a square, angular cloth on his head. There were about two hundred seats surrounding the middle of the room, forming some sort of an arena. About five or six gravely bored figures sat there, most likely young deacons.

'It is necessary for us to move beyond the conservatism of old sardonic priests...' roared one of the priests.

'It's started,' whispered Donna and pulled Grunt into one of the rows of seats. Five or six gravely bored faces turned to them for a second and then continued watching the boring scene.

'All right,' said a man on the other side of the table with a conciliatory voice, 'I admit the times change and the Bible could be translated into a more modern language and thus address today's rebel young. But I'd still urge preserving the meaning of the words so sacredly revealed in the Bible. So, even if the Lord may close his only eye and overlook changing "My name is Legion, for we are many" to "Yo, I'm the ant-hill cause there's shitloads of us", he would certainly send Plagues of Egypt for accepting Brother Damian's proposal for changing "Amen I say to you" to "Napoo, I yap you" and "Amen, Amen I say" to "Napoo already". I would also never support changing the words that our Lord said to Peter when he wavered in his faith from "Begone, Satan!" to "Piss off, jerk!" And this is only an example of Damian's heretical work. How many changes has Brother Damian made in the Bible, master Administrator?'

The addressed man consulted his notes and then answered: 'There are exactly three hundred and ninety two point five, not counting the cover with the name 'Ripper's Bible' on it and the...'

'Point five?' asked the conservative priest.

'Oh yes, master Scholastic. Master reformer made one weird change which we consider a print bug because otherwise it would condemn him to eternal damnation.'

'What weird change?'

'There is a sentence in Luke 23:24 when our Lord is already on the cross: "The soldiers played a game to see how they should divide his clothes." But Brother Damian's version says for some reason: "The soldiers played a game to see how they should divide his udder."'

'It wasn't me!' shouted Damian, terrified. 'It was Gregor!'

The man with the square cloth on his head looked disgusted: 'Is it true, Brother Gregor?'

'Yes, it is,' answered the man he'd addressed, 'and I won't waver in defending the truth!'

'So you do not disclaim this heresy?'

'Never!'

'Then thou shall be passed to the Cruel Inquisition!'

A man sitting next to him whispered few words into his ear.

'Again?' he asked quietly. 'Who is supposed to remember that? Oh, all right then,' he raised his voice again. 'We don't allow the terror of the Cruel Inquisition any more. Thou shall be passed to the Sacred Officium.'

'I'm aware of that.'

'Master Inquisitor, begin the trial.'

Another priest stood up. 'Brother Gregor, make a confession, in the face of God and the Congregation of the Doctrine of Faith."

'I believe in the Holy sixuality,' Gregor started, 'I declare the world is ruled by Father, Mother, Son, Daughter, Grandson and Granddaughter. And these six have six together all the time. The Eucharist is not needed for salvation but especially the Daughter's body brings bliss to the believer.'

Inquisitor lost patience: 'Your confession will lead you to eternal damnation!'

But Brother Gregor continued: 'The holy six is opposed by the unholy six B's. These are Boozer, Bawd, Bastard, Bitch, Bequestor and Booby. These try to snatch our souls.'

A man sitting next to him tried reasoning with him: 'But Brother Gregor, you can't mean this.'

Brother Gregor sneered at him: 'What can a Chaplain like you know about the true faith? I am the heretic here. Me! Because I'm the best!'

'Brother Gregor,' the Inquisitor reminded him. 'Art thou aware of pride being a deadly sin?'

'So what?!' he shouted at him. 'I'm the heretic here! Not just a poor babbling curator or a pervert judge wanking while reading testimonies of orgies in the mud with rats and frogs and wide anuses. I'm God and I know everything. Those who oppose me are Satan's minions!'

'Brother Gregor, you will be burned at the stake for this.'

'So be it!' Gregor yapped at him and smashed a glass on the table with his fist. The Chaplain went and cleaned up the mess. 'I'll be resurrected to smash your heads three days after that!'

'Brother Gregor, that is enough!'

'Shut your face, Asshole! I mean, Assbishop! Or I'll probe your pubis with your own staff!'

'You're sentenced then,' said the Inquisitor wearily, 'but could you, please, tell me why you changed the sentence in the Bible? What did you mean by dividing the Lord's udder?'

The heretic calmed down. 'Oh that... that is an irrelevant thing. I'd forgotten all about it. I believe our Lord Jesus died in India of natural causes.'

'Another heresy! Burn him!'

'Making a note,' said Administrator.

'Wait, Administrator,' the Inquisitor stopped him. 'I am the one who shall determine how many times the sinner shall be burned.'

The Reformer seemed nervous. 'Hey! You can't burn one heretic more than once.'

'For such a performance? Four times would be too few!'

'But... but that's not fair!'

'Be quiet, Reformer!' said the Inquisitor, 'or even thou shall stand the trial of the Bloody Inqui... I mean Officium.'

'But...' Brother Damian murmured something under his breath and stared at the table with an expression so foul that if the table had ever been able to breathe it had just breathed its last.

'Brother Gregor, please continue.'

'I will, your Gayness.'

'Then thou hast even lost respect for the tribunal?'

'I have, master Intestintor, the official of the highest Ofacilium.'

The Inquisitor was a little confused. 'Was that an insult?'

'The worst of all!' Brother Gregor assured him.

'This will mean another burning, you know that?'

'I can cope with that.'

'Tsss!' hissed the Reformer angrily.

'So, Brother Gregor, what about Jesus having an udder?'

'I think he was a cow,' answered Gregor simply.

'What? A cow? Why?'

'Well...' Gregor smiled slightly, 'have you seen anything else which managed to die of natural causes in India?'

To Grunt's amazement, everyone including Donna clapped frantically. The Administrator stood up and announced: 'The points have been counted and the person with the most, and who therefore becomes our new Pope is... Brother Gregor!'

Gregor stood up, approached the throne with a noble walk, accepted the square-angled cloth, and sat on the throne.

'Long live Gregor...' the Administrator paused. 'I'm afraid we haven't solved this problem yet. I can't inaugurate him. Because with the new Pope, I'm not an Administrator anymore. He has to name his new Administrator first.'

There was a serious discussion among the priests. Only Damian didn't join the discussion. He was just watching the new, self-satisfied pope with the deepest disgust on his face.

'Right then,' said the Administrator after a period of murmuring. 'The struggle for investiture has ended. We've agreed the Pope is elected by God so he first names his new Administrator who then names him and decides on the number for his name.'

The only one who seemed unsatisfied was Damian: 'I demand a new calculation!'

'A good idea, considering how many times Gregor has been the Pope. If we miscount we'd have to claim one of his previous Popes was the Anti-pope, and with that, of course, the Anti-pope would be a saint. And that would cause a lot of trouble...'

'I didn't mean that!' fumed Damian. 'I don't give a fuck how many times he was the Pope. I want a recount of the points!'

'Look, Damian,' the Administrator tried to console him, 'Gregor arranged three hundred and twenty burned heretics this month. It's a record in the modern history of church.'

'I made three hundred and eighty changes in the Bible, which is a record since its revision by the Lateran council.'

'I know. But most of them are repeated and some of them are total bullshit. Just accept this. You have been a strong opponent; he has just been better. But don't be downhearted. You may be the Pope the next month.'

'Sure,' Damian mumbled. 'Gregor hates me. He'll make me the Chaplain again!'

'I'm sure Brother Gregor is a godly person so he can't hate his fellow man. But now, he needs to name his new Administrator. I'd suggest we end this spiritual inter-regnum which damages the image of the church in the eyes of the public,' Grunt looked at Donna with an unspoken question of whether he was referring to the two of them, 'and get back to the official business. So, your Holiness,' he turned back to the Pope, 'name your new Administrator.'

'The new Administrator will be Brother Willfreak,' said Gregor patronizingly.

'Willfread, your Holiness' the new Administrator corrected him doubtfully, but stood up nevertheless and accepted a pergament and a feathered quill, the symbols of his ancient office. These tools had been used throughout history not only to record all the property donated by pious noblemen to the church, but also to poke out the eyes of pious noblemen who had been uncertain about where and when they'd exactly donated them.

'Long live Pope Gregor the thirty eight hundred and ninety-fifth!' announced the Administrator.

'What?' Grunt looked at Donna.'Have there been so many of them?'

'No,' Donna whispered back, 'but you need to understand that becoming the Pope twice in a row is not an easy task. You need to be really egoistic, historionicistic and insufferable to do that.'

'Why can't you just be nice and help others?'

'You can. But if you were, you'd have no chance of defeating those in the strong positions, like the Reformer or the Heretic. If the Pope wants to gain enough points he has to be as bad as possible. One month, Gregor secured the Papal post by making the Administrator inaugurate him repeatedly every minute he wasn't sleeping.'

'Even on the toilet?'

'Especially there.'

'What poor soul played the Administrator?'

'Guess,' smiled Donna slightly guiltily. 'Damian, of course. Those two really don't love each other.'

Meanwhile, the new Pope granted the offices with theatrical gestures. He even let the Anti-pope be taken from the prison. He hadn't expressed enough grievous sounds and prayers for Satan to win the contest although being the Anti-pope was usually a straight way to the top.

'And Damian, by the will of God and my office,' Gregor grimaced madly, 'will be the Chaplain.'

'I'll kill him!' shouted Damian and burst forward.

'Recording the first minus points,' said the Administrator calmly while Damian was being struck down and sentenced to death by burning.

'Be prudent,' smiled Gregor happily. 'It isn't so bad. You don't need to do much. And death by malnutrition is worth four hundred points. Oh yes, I nearly forgot. The Sacred Officium is now changed to the Brutal yet Righteous Unstoppable Tribunal for Achieving the Lord's Equitable Revenge. Its first task will be prosecuting Chaplains who are suspected of performing magic.'

The council ended and Grunt and Donna left the place.

'I think it's good for the church that Gregor has won,' said Donna happily. 'He's really strong.'

Grunt didn't answer.

'He's a great personality.'

Grunt was still quiet.

'Damian, of course, is good too...'

'Donna?'

'But when it comes to presenting the church...'

'Donna?'

'What?'

'I don't get it.'

'What?'

'Nothing.'

'And what exactly?'

'Nothing at all.'

'Could you be more specific?'

'Well... why do they do that?'

'Do what?'

'Why do they play at being the Inquisitor and Reformer and so on?'

'Isn't it obvious?'

'No, it isn't.'

'I don't see anything non-obvious about it.'

'Explain it, then.'

'I'm not sure if I can speak for them. I wouldn't like to misrepresent them.'

'Will you, please, answer me already?'

'I... well... sure, but why are you asking?'

'I've asked you first.'

'What?'

'I asked you why they do that.'

'You mean like playing the Reformer and Inquisitor and so on?'

'That's exactly what I've said already.'

'When?'

'Donna! Stop that! I know that game too. It works with Troglodyte but not with me. You know exactly what I mean.'

'Well,' Donna reddened slightly, 'I don't think they play it. They are the Reformer and the Inquisitor and so on.'

'And the Heretic? For a month?'

'Every church needs a heretic.'

'Sure but someone else. I believe there are many heretics in Zion.'

'Everyone there. But if the church burned them the humans would die out. And even if it wanted to burn anyone the heretics most probably wouldn't agree.'

'Exactly, Donna. It's stupid.'

'It certainly is not!'

'Why do they change roles every month?'

'To make it fair.'

'Doesn't Gregor or anyone as strong always win?'

'They earn the Pope's post through their abilities.'

'What is so great about being the Pope?'

Donna looked scandalized: 'What do you mean by that? The Pope is the ultimate authority. He is the supreme ruler.'

'Of what?'

'Of... of the world, I suppose.' Donna thought she should have played the 'what' game even though Grunt had forbidden it.

'Like Zion and the neighbouring sewers?'

'Well...' Donna was saying each word very slowly, probably hoping Grunt would lose his interest, 'that is a little problem.'

'Why?'

'Because the town council has never accepted Constantine's Donation.'

'What is that?'

'A document by which Constantine, an emperor who died a few thousand years ago,[25] granted the world to the church.'

'Did Constantine own the world?'

'He ruled its most significant part.'

'Ruled. But didn't own?'

'Of course not.'

'I see. So how big a part did he rule?'

'About five percent...'

'Five percent? That doesn't seem like a significant part to me.'

'But it was all the world they knew...'

'So he granted the world he didn't know about?'

'Grunt, what if I clank you with a shovel?'

'Why?' Grunt continued.

'Because you're annoying, that's why! Can't you just accept someone has granted the world?'

Grunt thought for a while. 'No,' he answered.

'Just accept it. The emperor Constantine granted the world to the church.'

'Why did he do that?'

'What?'

'Why did he grant the world to the church?'

'I don't know. Because he was so pious, probably. Anyway, the church now claims the right to rule over the world. Since the Pope is the highest member of the church he would be the world leader.'

'All right, then. Why does it not work in Zion?'

'Because the town council said they'd think about it when they actually see the document.'

'They don't have it?'

---

[25] I'm really good at hiding the date, am I not?

'Have I forgotten to mention it?' She put on an innocent face.

'So, if I understand well, the whole might of the church is based on a document no one has ever seen. A document by which thousands of years ago, for some reason, some bloke granted them the world which, if fact, didn't belong to him?'

'It sounds bad when you put it that way.'

'But is it like that?'

'Technically speaking...'

'What do you mean by "technically speaking"? Is it right or not?'

'The document existed. But the machines have taken it and copied it into the matrix.'

'Good. It was in the matrix, then.'

'It was but.... well... never mind.'

'Tell me. But what?'

'But they... they found out it was a fake.'

'A fake? You're kidding, right?'

'But it was the illusional one. If we find the real one it may as well be real.'

'What?' Grunt asked.

'I mean... oh, never mind.'

They continued on their way silently.

'Why didn't the church try to get something similar from anyone in Zion?' asked Grunt then, 'the sewers, for a start.'

'They did. They negotiated with Neo, offering to canonize him.'

'You mean shoot to pieces?'

Donna seemed angry: 'My God, Grunt! How can you speak about the essence of beingness for hours but not know the basic cultural terms? What about saints? Are they to be found on a beach?'

'I'm not sure I follow you.'

Donna calmed down. She realized her sarcasm had been very weak. 'Canonizing means making someone a saint.'

'I see. So they wanted to make him a saint if he donated something to them.'

'Exactly. Neo drew up the document "Neo's Donation" by which he granted Zion to the church.'

'But he hasn't been an owner of Zion, has he? Not even a ruler.'

'Mordeus said that he doesn't understand how a blind weirdo can grant anything, and certainly not Zion.'

'How did the church react?'

'They declared an interdict on him.'

'What is an interdict?' he asked warily. He might not survive the next attack of beach-related sarcasm.

'When an interdict is declared on something you can't perform any church rituals there. Like burials or weddings.'

'Would anyone want that? Perform burials in Mordeus?'

'It's actually an example of how the church's power is futile. They wanted to declare the interdict on the whole city. But the Grave committee opposed that strongly because even without the interdict people don't want to bury anyone much. And since the Grave committee is more powerful than the church, the priests had to recall the interdict and call it on Mordeus only. We met a joker once who said cheekily to Gravefiller that his dead friend had written a will in which he had stated clearly he wanted to be buried in Mordeus. And since it was no longer possible, the burial couldn't take place.'

'Did you explain to him the errors in his argument?'

'No.'

'Why not?'

'It's hard to explain anything to a corpse.'

'I see,' Grunt nodded. 'I'd forgotten he said it to Gravefiller. Why is the Grave committee so powerful?'

'Because everyone fears it.'

'So why doesn't the Grave committee rule instead?'

'Can you imagine a society driven by fear?'

'Well enough. In fact, I don't recall any society driven by anything else.'

'But the Grave committee... they're... they're scum. Garbage. The worst of the worst. Nobody wants to do that job.'

'So how can it be so powerful?'

'Because when you've fallen so low you can do anything. That's why you have power. But imagine the laws. Murder won't be considered a crime. But everything else would. Old people would have to attend "anonymous-corpses" meetings. Mandatory savings to cover death expenses would be required.'

'I'm starting to feel you don't like being a grave-digger at all,' concluded Grunt.

'Look, Grunt, if I was a man I could have been a priest. I tried to persuade them they needed a nun. But they've got that democratic system of theirs so they were afraid they might end up as nuns instead. Absolute macho tyrants these guys are! I told them I'd do it permanently. They told me I'm a fanatic and threw me out.'

'So why did you join the Grave committee? You should have had many other opportunities.'

'Like what? I tried to be a hairdresser. But my first customer tried to commit suicide with curling tongs after about half an hour talking with me. That was when the Grave committee noticed me for the first time. Then, I was a shopkeeper in a food shop. A real luxury one. Fried rats, concrete worms, a green goo from... whatever it was. Anyway, the people seemed to like me. They spent hours with me, talking. They told me they remembered me every time they ate.'

'What went wrong then?'

'They all died of malnutrition.' Donna seemed to be on the verge of tears. 'They were all anorexics. They connected me with food so they never wanted to eat again. And they succeeded. When anyone tried to make them eat something they started crying and their white faces were full of an immense terror.' The first tears started pouring from her eyes. He knew he should do something. After all, his questions were the reason she was crying.

'You don't scare me at all,' he tried saying, but it didn't help in any way. He had to add more emotions, 'On the contrary, I really enjoy talking with you.'

'Oh, Grunt!' Donna screamed and she thrust herself around his neck.

It was good. It was more than good. It was very, very good. Grunt never did anything like that to him. And Donna seemed to be so experienced at it...

'Have you ever considered becoming a prostitute?' The words slipped out. It was too late to correct the mistake.

Donna now went into uncontrollable sobs: 'Who... who to-told you?' she hiccupped, 'it was Troglodyte, wasn't it?'

'Well... I...' Grunt tried to find a way out of this.

'I just said that. I've never actually done it.'

'Why haven't you?'

Again, this wasn't the right thing to say. Donna was on the verge of collapsing.

'After the dead anorexics, the Grave committee offered me a job at last. I told them I'd rather be a whore. But someone spread the word and... and,' she cried even more, 'all the who-whores lost all their cli-clients.'

'Why?'

'Because the-they tho-thought any of them may b-be me. The horny guys melted away from the streets so no honest woman could be sure she'd be honest the next day. Especially when the store selling sedatives was robbed. The family members took revenge on the rapists and there was a b-b-blood bath in Zion. The Grave committee offered me a job again. I was so depressed I accepted.'

'I understand, I'd be depressed too. After so many deaths...' He hoped she might hug him again if he showed enough understanding.

'Screw the dead!' she surprised him. 'I was depressed because everyone had been so intellectually retarded. Not only didn't they know the difference between Kant and cunt but they even hated you when you tried to explain it. But everything has changed now. Because you are here...' With these words she flung her arms around his neck again. He started thinking about getting more information about those sedatives. 'There are two of us intellectuals now. The oppressed will rise and gain glory. Intellect will spread from graveyards to lead the society on the right path, the path to truth and enlightenment!'

'And Donna?' Grunt asked tenderly while stroking her hair.

'Yes?'

'Are you sure you're not a fanatic?'

The last question wasn't the right one to ask at all. Donna got offended and went off angrily. Grunt had a lot to learn about human emotions. If someone gives you a hand you don't bite it. Especially when it seems she may give more. Head, for example. But this was another of Grunt's problems. He knew absolutely nothing about what to do if Donna had actually given him more. He hadn't expected this at all. He thought he'd solve these problems with his hulk wife slowly. But she simply refused to cooperate with his attempts to find a compatible interface. She may have had a good reason though since his last experiment ended with her nose being broken. From inside. What if the same mistakes happened with Donna as well? He also realized he'd missed some very important lessons while working in the Section. He'd always read something about the right positions, sizes, right humidity and a lot of other agricultural values. But Donna's hug felt more like sex than anything he'd tried with Grunt. He was confused and scared he may screw it up as he'd screwed it up with Grunt. If anyone would just explain it to him!

And there were many problems apart from sex, although much less important ones. He wasn't sure what to think about the Donation of Constantine. Was there really some sort of a forged document, hidden in the city of machines? And had the machines really made that great effort to copy it into the matrix? After all, those idiots would certainly process it and mark it as a new weapon or a luxury food. How could machines have made a matrix anyway? They didn't understand human behaviour even a little bit. How could they have created something they did not understand, and do it so well that those who did understand would not find a flaw?

While walking through the dark streets of Zion at night, thinking hard about church and sex, he approached a dark (well, darker, anyway) archway. He remembered a film he'd seen in the Section and thought that if this situation had been in a film he would be ambushed any time now. He laughed at the idea and started singing silently a dramatic melody he'd heard in such scenes.

'Dam-dam-tu-du-du-dum,' Grunt sang as he went through the archway,

'Dam-dam-tu-du-du-dum,' he went through without being ambushed,

'Dam-dam-tu-du-du-dum,' it was good. The funny thought made his mind slip away from Donna and the machines.

'Dam-dam...' a small group appeared at the corner of the street.

'tu-du-du-dum.'

The group surrounded him.

'Yo, chick! Show what you got under the bonnet,' one of them said.

Grunt tried to find the meaning of the sentence for few seconds. Then, he just gave up.

'Is this an ambush?' he asked simply.

The men looked at each other. 'What do you think?' the leader hissed through his teeth.

'I'm not sure,' answered Grunt calmly. 'So what about yes?'

'Right.'

'That's great!' Grunt was excited by his new discovery. 'So it works like that for humans.'

'What?'

'I mean... us humans. You are humans, right?'

'What?'

'I just found out. Do you know why I was singing Dam-dam-tu-du-du-dum?'

The speaker pressed him against the wall. Grunt didn't like it. Something wasn't entirely right.

'Why?' the aggressor exposed his teeth.

'Well... because... uhm... excuse me, could you loosen your grip on my neck a little bit, please? It's very hard to speak when you're doing it.'

The aggressor was so confused he actually loosened it.

'Better, thank you,' Grunt pretended to be cool and fine but he felt actually more and more nervous every second. 'I was singing it because I thought it went with the situation when a bloke like me is ambushed. But in fact, it causes them.'

'Could you repeat that?'

'I sang it because I thought it went with the situation when a bloke like me...'

'A bloke like you?!'

'Yes...'

'You surely mean, a chick like you, right?!' the guy looked as if he might get very nasty soon. Grunt thought hard. Perhaps if one kind of melody led him in, some other may lead him out. He tried to find something in his memory.

'I asked you a question!'

'Hush-a-bye, baby, don't cry...' sang Grunt.

'What?!'

'I'm a little teapot...'

'What are you gaggling about?'

'You are my sunshine...'

His face was hit by an uncomfortably hard fist. Singing obviously didn't work. Perhaps all these situations needed special preparation, Grunt thought. But what to do now?

'You shouldn't hurt me.' All right, it was pretty lame. But it might grant him few more seconds while he thought of something better.

'Why?' A few more seconds were gone.

'Because... because we should join...'

'That's exactly what we intend to do, baby!' roared the aggressor.

'...against the common enemy.'

'And who is that, honey?'

'Machines, of course!'

Grunt expected they'd look at each other, feel the sudden blast of solidarity with the whole of humanity and agree with him. Instead, they all started crying with laughter.

'Are you telling me,' one of them asked, laughing, 'you actually buy that stuff?'

'What? What stuff? I don't buy anything...'

'That's bullshit the ruling class uses to keep the working class and the under-working class under control!'

'I'm not sure I follow.'

'The machines don't exist!'

Humanity is often misguided. It is misguided in not believing in God's existence, in burning witches at stakes in the name of the non-existing God, in electing the Bushy George as the ruler of the world's strongest super nation, or bulldozer.[26] But no one insists on telling God in a face-to-face chat that he doesn't, in fact, exist.[27]

'Don't exist?' The words came from Grunt's dry mouth.

'They don't.'

'I've seen them. And my wife too.'

'So you're a lesbo?'

'What?'

'A lesbo!'

'What is a lesbo?'

The aggressor seemed unsure if he should be amazed or just violent. Nevertheless, he answered: 'A lesbian, a chick who licks a chick.'

---

[26] Some of you may feel offended now but I don't mean the vehicle itself*. I mean the name. Why is a building tool named 'a light-sleeping ox'? What similarity is there? Or does it refer to its driver? Are the bulldozerers big rutting oafs who regularly fall asleep while driving, smashing the whole blocks of building into pieces before being woken? And then, wouldn't drivers who are boring and drink too much be called 'Dullboozers'? Can you imagine how the bulldozer drivers must be... well... bullied?

*A bulldozer, of course, is a very usefull tool which increases the luxury level of all who participate in the fruits of the bulldozer's work. Naturally not if a shortsighted dullboozerer starts his duty too early and drives across a field on which a party of christian pilgrims fell asleep the previous night.**

**Oh, sorry, that is a harvester.

[27] Well, the members of the Committee for Sceptical Inquiry may. But they'd lie in a den of badly fed zombies, claiming zombies don't exist. They'd probably claim they didn't believe in the existence of humans the next morning.

'But chicks can't lick each other, can they? They don't have tongues.'

The aggressor hit him again. 'I will rip out your tongue and show it to you so you can see that chicks have tongues!'

'I'm not a chick...'

'What?! Are you telling me you're not a female?'

'How do you identify one?'

They looked at each other without a word for a while. Then, the aggressor realized he'd lost the initiative absolutely.

'When I stick my dick in your hole, you'll identify that!'

Grunt's brain came to the right conclusion finally: 'You want sex?'

The guys looked at each other, confused: 'Sure. What did you think?'

'And will you show me how to do that?' Grunt started a new adventure.

It confused the gangbang leader so much he tried to gain some time to think: 'Where did you see them?'

'Who?'

'The machines.

'It doesn't matter,' Grunt waved his hand. 'Show me how to make sex. You know, like what you insert in what. I want to try it with my wife then.'

'So you are a lesbian?'

'Sure, why not?' Grunt was unhappy it took so long.

'But a female doesn't have anything to insert.'

'And how many possibilities are there?'

'What possibilities?

'I mean types.'

'What types?' the aggressor started panicking. Even he now felt something was wrong. He'd expected the usual plot - some macho speeches, a little necessary violence, sex and rest. But suddenly the world he knew felt apart.

'I mean, is there any other type than a male and a female?'

'No...' the party leader answered desperately.

'I see. No problem then. My wife has more to insert than I do.'

'Your wife is a bloke?' Clearly, the group would love to escape, just to have a good excuse.

'Yeah, it seems so.'

The aggressor came to his senses at last: 'Guys! That chick is only playing with us. Let's give her...'

An ironing board fell on his head.

The other party members watched their leader, lying on the ground, knocked out. Then, they decided there may not be any better excuse. They ran off.

'Hey!' Grunt shouted after them. 'You promised me...'

'Young lady,' a voice came from above. Grunt looked up. An old woman with something that resembled a ring net on the top of her head was gazing short-sightedly from a window on the third floor.

'Young lady, please, can you see my ironing board anywhere there? It just fell out of my window.'

'I can,' Grunt answered. 'Do you want me to bring it to you?'

'It would be very sweet of you, darling,' the old woman croaked with a voice which was meant to make her sound even older and show she didn't have such young feet as Grunt had and that if she'd had to bring the board herself she might end up lying on one.

'And will you show me how to make sex?' Grunt shouted. After a minute of tactful silence a soft but less croaking voice said: 'Bring me the ironing board, darling, will you?'

For a few minutes, Grunt thought about how to take the ironing board in a logical way. Since he couldn't think of a good way he just dragged the board behind him up the stairway. Very soon, the face of a very upset man looked out from a door on the first floor.

'Who the hell is making that fucking noise?!' he shouted. It seemed he was going to become evil very soon. Grunt didn't have the strength for another conflict today so he tried saying the first thing which crossed his mind: 'This is the Grave committee,' he shouted. 'We've received a message there is an unburied corpse in the house.'

It was a really good idea. The man's face changed in a second from a berserker bear to a cute little teddy-bear of a pastel colour who said, in a 'Laa-Laa wants a Big hug' type of voice: 'I am so happy you're here. I won't bother you,' and he disappeared behind the door again, probably leaving the house by a window immediately after that.

'He seems he has already met Gravefiller,' he thought. 'From a distance, of course,' he added since the man had seemed to be moving, speaking and breathing, so he had definitely been alive. Grunt continued on his way up the stairs in the same fashion as before he'd been interrupted, making a noise like a pair of mating hippos in a pottery store.

The owner of the ironing board greeted him at the door, noticeably shaking. She obviously wasn't sure if Grunt's proclamation had been true but the mere mention of the Grave committee made people tremble. If it hadn't been so hard to purchase a good ironing board in Zion those days she would certainly have played... well... played alive, but behind the door.

'You seem so experienced in carrying boards,' she said cunningly, although the way Grunt did it was anything but experienced.

'Really?' Grunt was shining with happiness. 'You won't believe I didn't know how to carry it at all at the beginning.'

'Oh,' the woman seemed much more relaxed. 'So you don't carry boards often, Darling?' she smiled convulsively.

'No, I don't,' he smiled in the same manic way. When the woman showed him in, he continued doing so because he thought it was some sort of a ritual, 'they always make me carry shovels.'

The unnatural smile on the woman's face froze, which made it even more unnatural than it had been before. She looked at Grunt's blank expression and his horrible grin, which Grunt considered was friendly but which seemed to her to be a psychopathic sign, then at the board still in his hand.

'Do-don't y-you want to pu-put that down?' she stammered.

'Now?' said Grunt who still wasn't thinking about anything else but sex.

'Pa-pa-pardon?'

'I mean, I'm not sure I want it here, in the doorway where anyone could see it.'

The woman's horror vision seemed to come true: 'W-why?'

'I don't know. I just think these things should be more discreet. I even think the society may prosecute me for that if anyone sees us.'

'If y-you hurt me they will, even if no one sees you. But y-you do-don't want to hurt me, d-do you, h-ha ha,' she laughed in a horrible squeaky voice.

'It may happen, I think,' Grunt really didn't know. Last time, he'd broken Grunt's nose. And that could certainly be considered as 'hurting someone'.

'You aren't planning to do anything to me with the board, are you?' she laughed in the same horrible squeaky voice again.

'Is it possible?' Grunt thought about the board's metal feet.

'Put the board down, p-please,' she tried saying, even though she knew it was very feeble.

'The board? Oh, of course. It belongs to you, doesn't it?'

'Great, thank you. And now... excuse me, I need to...' she tried to get rid of the visitor.

'Will we go in?' Grunt didn't give her a chance.

'G-go in?'

'Sure. I told you already, I don't want to do it now.'

'But I...' she was speechless but she knew she had to find something quickly. 'There is no corpse here.' Let me point out the woman's voice didn't sound as croaky and weary as it had before. This was a voice of a vital middle-age woman who may still have many years of life ahead.

'I don't want a corpse.'

'No? But what do you want then?'

'You.'

The woman calculated her chances. The window on the fourth floor, an enemy in the doorway and the only possible weapon is in the enemy's hand. She had to negotiate. 'Are you sure you wouldn't prefer a corpse?'

Grunt considered that for a while. If you look at a problem logically you may resolve it better. But then he remembered Donna's hug.

'Definitely not,' he answered.

'But-but why not?'

'Because there won't be any interaction, no personal relation. Just wham, wham and finished. Not even a moan.'

'Do you need your victim to moan?'

'I prefer the term "partner" if you don't mind.'

'I won't moan at all.'

'Positive?'

'Positive.

'Pity. But never mind. Some people are completely silent during the act. It can still be good.'

'I-I will shout if you...'

'Great!' the image made Grunt even more horny, 'Great! So let's stop talking and let's do it!'

The woman had reached a dead end in her negotiations: 'Please... I don't wanna.'

Grunt lowered his head sadly: 'Positive?'

'Positive.'

'Are you absolutely sure about that?'

'I am.'

Grunt nodded. 'All right then. I can't force you.' Then, all the uncertainty and stress of the last days came over him and he burst into tears. Among the sobs, he said things like: 'Why am I so unlucky?' or 'Why does everyone dismiss me?' After a while, even the woman felt sorry for him and tried consoling him. She realized she was no longer in trouble since the maniac obviously needed permission from his victims.

'Don't cry,' she tried, 'I believe one day you'll find someone who will be willing to let you do away with him or her.'

'I won't. Even my wife doesn't let me.'

'Doesn't she really? Well, what can you do? You can't force her,' she realized how absurd the situation was.

But there was no consoling Grunt. 'And they come with some stupid dotation or whatever and they all call me a female... and... and...'

'Don't you want a cup of tea, Darling?'

Grunt nodded. 'And will you at least tell about sex?'

'Sure, I will,' she thought she should add something. 'And if you want I will show you some photos.'

Grunt stopped crying abruptly. 'Photos? Really? Photos of inserting into the holes?'

'Pardon m...' but then she realized his expression was changing from hopelessness to happiness, 'of course.'

And then she just added: 'And are you sure you don't want to put the board down?'

When Grunt had left the nice woman he had all the necessary knowledge. He knew everything about sex, at least theoretically. And since he didn't yet know how far the theory and practice were different he felt really confident. As an irony of fate, when he turned the corner two barely clothed figures crossed his path. One of them looked at his face and shouted: 'Kristeen! You alive! That's wonderful!' and she thrust herself around his neck. Today was a really good day.

'I'm not Kristeen, I'm Grunt,' he said after enjoying himself for some time, when the woman loosened her hug at last.

'What?' she asked.

'I'm not Kristeen, I'm Grunt.'

'What are you blabbing about? Course you are Kristeen. I'm Deepbra. And this is Syphyllis,' the other woman waved. 'You don't remember me? How many times we were blowing together...'

He thought about the last time he and Gravefiller had had those chilli beans from a replicator. He wasn't sure there was anything exciting about blowing together. But while he was considering this, some other feelings and memories which didn't belong to him appeared in his head. They were blurred but he was sure they were even worse than the first idea of co-blowing.

'I'm not Kristeen. I'm Grunt,' but then he decided to show off a little, 'but I know everything about sex.'

'Sure you do,' said Syphillis with enthusiasm, 'you've nibbled more sticks than either of us.'

'No, I'm pretty sure about this. I haven't nibbled any sticks in my life.'

'Of course you have! You are the best at it. All those poor guys hired you for the highest prices. Here, look,' she took a small notebook from her pocket. 'I took it to remember you. They told us you'd been killed.'

Grunt took the notebook. It was full of names, dates, lengths, prizes and occasional notes such as 'jerk', 'boss', 'cutie' or 'bulldozer'. There was the following statement on the first page:

'STEP 1: Find da poorest blowk.

STEP 2: Gif him dee ekstasy

STEP 3: Teyk all he has.'
'Hey, that has more grammar errors than an English book written by a Czech writer!'
The women looked at each other, confused: 'What? Did they brainwash you?'
'Why a poor man? Why not a rich one?'
'Because of the taxes, of course. Kristeen, you can't have forgotten everything!'
'I am not Kristeen, I'm Grunt. Explain.'
'Come with us, we will show you everything.'
He scanned both their bodies. 'You already have,' he looked at Deepbra's face: 'Please, tell me here and now.'
'All right, then. When Zion was founded a law was passed to make rich people pay higher taxes than the poor. But since there was never too much money, the Town council considered everyone rich after some time. Except those who were rich enough to pay a bribe to have themselves listed as poor.[28]'
'Corruption then?'
'Co... what?'
'That's disgusting.'
'Of course it is. So do you remember?'
Some images came from the fog of his memory. And he didn't like them. He didn't want to be a barely clothed woman in this cold weather, especially when she was so poor she had to eat sticks. The den of the Grave committee was really bad but there was still mud from a replicator. He didn't have to eat wood.
He took the notebook and, using great grammar and a tidy font, he wrote a few words in it. Then he left without

---

[28] Do you think this is an unrealistic vision created by the author's diseased mind? Have you ever lived in a communist country?

a word. It took a while before the women read it. It said: 'Thanks for your willingness to help me but I don't need you. I am not Kristeen, I'm Grunt. I'm a member of the Grave committee. Don't search for me and I won't search for you.'

He finally understood what the power of the Grave committee was based on.

Grunt came back to the den. The first person he met was Donna, who didn't speak to him, obviously angry with him for telling her she was a fanatic. When he entered the hole he met Grunt who didn't speak to him either. And when he'd met himself and found out that even himself was not speaking to him he slammed his head against the wall and fell asleep.

Some time ago, he had read on a fire-prevention sign somewhere in the depths of Zion that an alarm could be announced by 'long hitting to metal items'. He remembered this because he couldn't imagine how to make a 'long hit'. But the noises which woke him up in the middle of the night could be described exactly like that. Although it could mean anything in the den of the Grave committee, beginning with Gravefiller banging shovels around, continuing with Skeleton under an automatic guillotine, ending with Donna building a bookcase. That's why he just rolled over. Unfortunately, by doing that, he made contact with the moustache of his wife, which woke him up immediately. He didn't know why but he felt something was terribly wrong.

Nevertheless, even if he hadn't woken up himself he'd have been woken up by Ferret who burst into the room, jumped on the straw bed and started to sniff Grunt's crotch. Ferret's moustache was even more unpleasant than his wife's. Troglodyte went after Fat rat and said: 'Yo, get up! You can't miss the fun.' Gravefiller was standing behind him, banging a shovel for some reason.

'What fun?' asked Grunt sleepily.

'There is an alert. A catastrophe of some kind. Mordeus will make some of his stupid speeches. And there will surely be a tekno after that. You don't want to miss it.'

'A lot of people will be trampled out in the crowd,' Gravefiller added with a dreaming expression.

Grunt still didn't want to get out of bed. 'What catastrophe?'

'Dunno,' said Troglodyte 'Probably a coming of the Gravefiller.' He laughed. Gravefiller hit him with a shovel in a friendly way[29].

'All right. And really?'

'I've told you. Not a clue,' answered Troglodyte and kicked Gravefiller's genitals in a friendly way. Since Gravefiller was always aroused by the prospect of burying, Troglodyte nearly crippled his leg.

'Could it be a machine raid?'

'Maybe. Or a flood. An earthquake?'

'Or a raid of rat locusts,' added Gravefiller. 'Last time it was like who'd be more hungry, us or them. Well, we were.'

'Yeah, those were rich times,' said Troglodyte and licked his lips[30]. 'So are you going or what?'

The gathering around the podium was getting bigger and bigger. A black guy who, accordingly to

---

[29] A non-lethal one.
[30] Not Gravefiller's. His own.

Troglodyte, was Mordeus ascended to it and started his speech: 'To all citizens of a happy and free democratic Zion...' While he was saying this Grunt had the feeling that all the surrounding reality sneered ironically. 'I am here to tell you the whole truth. A huge army of machines is approaching our city.'

A murmur and few hysterical shouts rose up from the crowd. A few ladies fainted. Also, a man in one of the further rows fainted, but it was hard to tell if it happened due to the terrible news or due to the terrible shovel held by Gravefiller, who was standing behind him.

'But don't panic. Although they outnumber us gravely and although they may crush every little bone in all our tiny fleshy bodies we are not afraid! Are you with me?'

'Yeah!' the crowd cheered.

'Because we are the civilization!

'Yeah!'

'We are the culture!'

'Yeah!'

'We are...'

'total idiots,' finished Donna silently.

'bold...' Mordeus continued.

'How did we stop the last raid?' a feeble voice came from somewhere in the crowd.

'We are strong!'

'Hey, I was asking something.'

'We are...'

'Once more, Mordeus, how did we stop the last raid?'

The crowd went silent. It could no longer ignore the rebel. It stopped chanting stage-managed slogans such as: 'Order us, leader!', 'Long live Mordeus' and 'When the hell are you going to turn the tekno on?'

Mordeus looked at the rebel: 'I'm not sure I understand your question,' he tried saying, hoping the rebel's self-preservation instinct might be strong enough to make him retract his question. It obviously wasn't.

'You told us a month ago tens of thousands of machines were going to reach Zion and that there was no way to stop them. And then, nothing. What happened?'

It was pretty sure the man's fate had been decided when he said the last word. The Gravefiller approached him but his well used shovel had to wait until the man was no longer at the centre of the crowd's attention.

His sacrifice was in vain. Mordeus was clever enough to find an answer. He looked over the crowd and said: 'Do you want to know how the last raid ended?'

Some answers flew out of the crowd, like: 'Tell us, leader,' 'We don't care' and 'Turn the tekno on already!'

'I will tell you how.'

'Speak, leader,' 'We believe you,' 'Tekno!'

'The machines didn't finish their attack because...'

An absolute silence fell.

'...They ran out of gas.'

A happy murmur went through the crowd. Gravefiller was faking a panicking crowd again and Grunt who'd forgotten to keep his lips sealed, said: 'But machines don't run on gas.'

He didn't say it too loudly. Even if he had, it would have been swallowed up in a mixture of drums and various industrial sounds that filled the square. Unfortunately, he said it loudly enough to make two pairs of hands grab him and drag him off.

Under normal circumstances, he'd be followed by his second part and Grunt. But now, both of them were looking awestruck at the square, which had now changed into a hellish dance floor. While they were listening to the sounds of a well equipped machine shop, watching the convulsive movements performed by citizens of all ages they both thought one thing: it is quite understandable when machines try to be like humans. But why on Earth do humans try to be like machines?

When the industrial sounds had ended, the citizens of Zion started their preparations for the attack. Mordeus and the other members of the town council gave weapons to the town militia. Women, children and cowards crawled to their holes and the Grave committee members were smiling madly at the thought of an imminent profit. Troglodyte especially urged them to remember soldiers saying goodbye to their families to ensure the families wouldn't deny them when they were dead. Grunt, Grunt and Donna (being women, children or cowards) took shelter in the Zion dockyard.

The positions were occupied in time because as soon as the last soldier took the handle of his mashing-gun[31] a small piece of plaster came unstuck from the ceiling.

'The mantinels are attacking!' shouted the general. A few very confused mantinels flew into the dockyard through the small hole in the ceiling. They had obviously gone completely haywire.

---

[31] No, I didn't mean a machine-gun. A machine-gun shoots bullets, while the mashing-gun mashes them. I agree the second one may be much more useful in a fight. But what do you know about the technology that will prove useful in the future? Jules Verne may have been ridiculed too when his Captain Nemo explored the ocean depths.

'Fire!' the general shouted and all the mashing-guns roared. The mantinels were destroyed in a few seconds, together with the main dock, docked ships and the control tower.[32]

'We have won,' the general summarized the battle, which had been full of dramatic scenes and unexpected events.

'Sir, something is approaching, sir,' an operator announced.

'What?' asked the general, breathing heavily.

'Sir, it looks like a ship, sir.'

'What ship?'

'Sir, our ship, sir.'

'Then it must be a provocation!'

'Sir, it's the Knocker, sir!'

'Can't be. Who's flying it?'

'Sir, Neo, sir!'

'The blind one?'

'The one with black glasses. Sir, yes, sir!'

'Then it really is a provocation.'

'Why? I mean... sir, why, sir?'

'Who has ever seen a blind man flying a ship?'

'Sir, he's the Chosen one, sir!'

'Oh, sure,' the general said ironically, 'the Chosen one. The whole of Zion has chosen him.'

'Sir, exactly my point, sir!'

'I mean the *whole* of Zion. Each pillar of Zion has met him already.'

'Sir, it isn't nice to make fun of him, sir. With all due respect, sir.'

'If he just bought himself a cane he'd save us a lot of trouble. Anyway, blind or not, now he's flying through a

---

[32] All right, all right, I meant a machine-gun.

ventilation duct. Even the sharpest beholder won't be
able to survive that.'
'Sir, he'll manage it...'
The ship exploded.
'Or not, sir!' the operator finished fluently.

Let's get back to Grunt 2. He was caught by
somebody, a gag was put into his mouth and he was
dragged out of the square. He tried to scream for help,
which explained why he had been given the gag. He
turned around to see his kidnappers. That he regretted
immediately. A situation when you are dragged through
streets by two pairs of ogre hands can make you feel
uneasy on its own. You don't need to add the discovery
that the two pairs of ogre hands actually belong to dirty
one-eyed ogres with evil expressions on something which
you'd call their faces only because of their location. Since
Grunt hadn't seen a common policeman before he
wondered if these could have been those brown rats
Troglodyte had been speaking about.

He was dragged into a dark room where a few
people were sitting in shadows. The only one clearly
visible and known to Grunt was Mordeus.[33] The ogres

---

[33] There is a theory that our light sensitivity is diverse. That what
we see as darkness is light and vice versa. It would explain why
cockroaches run through the room crazily when you turn the light
on and why they are trying to get back to their sunny sewer pipes.
Neverteless, although we are such terrible ignorants who blunder
in the light and try to defeat it by non-effective dark-bulbs and
cover the Earth with our cities' luminous smog which can be seen
even from the lightness of space we can sometimes behold the
true reality. Mostly when eating some slightly poisonous
compound or being in a mentally tough situation. And the
situation Grunt was in was so mentally tough there couldn't be

viciously threw him into a chair and finally released the gag. Grunt didn't know what to say. So he didn't say anything.

After few minutes of threatening silence, Mordeus said:

'They told me the young lady was a little too clever.'

Grunt thought frantically. What was he talking about? A clever young lady? Did he mean Donna? Was he down on Donna for her philosophy? Or did she actually say something clever? But why did they drag him out and not her? Nevertheless, he decided to defend her.

'I think she just babbles,' he answered.

'Really? Did she babble anything about machines?'

'I don't think so.'

'Punch her,' said Mordeus to one of his ogres. Grunt's face was hit.

'Tut tut, Mordeus,' a man in a shadow said. 'We are not hitting ladies, are we?'

Mordeus acted like he hadn't heard anything. 'They told me she was saying something about machines not running on gas.'

'It wasn't her,' Grunt boldly decided to clear Donna with his confession, 'it was me.'

Mordeus thought for a while to understand the meaning of the latest sentence. He gave up; it was too demanding for him. 'Punch her,' he just ordered. An ogre obeyed the order.

'Do you confess then?'

'I do,' said Grunt.

'Then tell me where did you get such information from, young lady?'

anything clearer for him than a blackman in a tunnel.

Grunt's brain combined the necessary information at last: 'Hey, I'm not a female. I'm a male.'

Mordeus looked at him with a very ugly expression: 'You mean a shemale?'

'What?'

'A shemale. Tranny. A bloke remade to a female?'

Grunt smiled. Someone understood it at last: 'Yes, exactly. A shemale.'

'Punch him!' Mordeus ordered. 'Shemales make me sick! Imagine it looks like a chick but it has a screwdriver dangling down there!'

'Where?'

They were watching each other cautiously, trying to determine who was actually winning.

'An easy test,' said Mordeus at last. 'Tell me how long that is,' and he indicated with his fingers a length of some six inches.

'About six inches,' Grunt answered.

'He's right, he's a bloke. Punch him.'

Grunt liked Mordeus less and less.

'Do you mean you can tell what gender I am by the fact I can figure out six inches?'

'Sure.'

'What would a female say, then?

'Between nine and twelve.'

'All of them?'

'All of them.'

'Mordeus, I really think you are an uneducated macho tyrant. You can't truly suppose manhood and womanhood is anything substantial. Why do you think a woman can't estimate length properly?'

'Punch him!'

'Don't think you can solve everything by violence! I want an answer!'

'I didn't say women can't estimate lengths. But they can't figure out six inches.'

'Why is that?'

'I'm starting to think you may be a woman after all. A male would know that.'

'Ha! So you've caught yourself! If I'm a male I should figure out six inches but I should also know the reason why females can't. You've got a paradox here. You should claim your theory as a falsum.'

'Punch him. And again.'

'You are not very good at conversation!'

Mordeus approached Grunt and bent down with a devilish smile. 'You are damn right. I'm not good at conversation. Because I don't need to be. I ask questions, you answer! Now tell me, do you have a screwdriver there?'

Mordeus was so close that Grunt started to think that he might get the chance to hurt him. His hands were bent but maybe if he bounced off the chair hard enough he might be able to bite Mordeus' neck artery...

'Answer the question!' yelled Mordeus. Grunt lost his nerve and remained sitting.

'I... I don't... I don't know anything about a screwdriver. I'm a male. Though my name, Grunt, could be dual-gender I consider myself as male.'

Mordeus stopped dead when he heard the name. He took a few steps back in a complete silence. Grunt's spirit was now somewhere under the floor. 'Mordeus knows,' he thought. What fate awaits him as a machine? Will they mash him with a mashing-gun, like the poor mantinels in the docks?

A few minutes later though, Mordeus spoke finally into the heavy silence. There was a trace of an evil grin on his face.

'I'll tell you what. Let's screw the gas business. You may just have been babbling as you said. I like the bravery that you've shown me. On the other hand, you've committed a crime by opposing me. Do you want to live? There is your choice. I want you to join the matrix soldiers.'

'Can I really choose?'

'Go ahead!'

'So, if I can really choose, I'd like to live but I don't want to be a matrix soldier.'

'That option is not on the table!'

'You told me I can choose.'

'Yeah, between the matrix and death.'

'But the question was phrased differently.'

'Don't play with me or I'll choose for you. Your last chance, mate: we will either kill you or you will join the matrix soldiers.'

'Oh, it's something completely different, then. You should express yourself clearly. That's important. Even your speech at the square...'

'Put a gun to his temple!'

Grunt 2 felt the cool touch of a steel barrel.

'Matrix then,' he answered quickly.

It wasn't that bad after all. They let him sleep on a real bed which didn't hurt his back and they gave him food which didn't hurt his mouth. Yes, he was a prisoner, but he had a better life than ever before when he'd been a free man. After all, if the east European socialistic experiment has been accompanied by high welfare you'd be reading this book in Russian now. Grunt's feelings were uncertain but he had no reason to rebel against his oppressors.

'Let's go, Grunt,' said Mordeus the next day. 'Your training starts in a few minutes.'

'How many minutes, exactly?' Grunt couldn't resist the urge to needle Mordeus.

'Exactly the number of minutes that are needed to get into the headquarters.'

'Great! So if I just got into Zion meanwhile...'

'I'd shoot you.'

'You would?'

'I would.'

Grunt's last sentence was meant to buy more time while he thought of a really acid answer. But the time was gone and it seemed Mordeus had won this time, thanks to his position of power, not his cleverness, of course. Sure, some bold comments such as 'You wouldn't dare' or 'You'd miss anyway' came to Grunt's mind but even his ego wasn't strong enough to make him say anything that stupid.

'Yo, Toluene,' Mordeus called a man in the corner who was, for some reason, covering his face with a scarf and a plastic bag, 'put that crap down or I'll shoot you. We are going to train a rookie.'

Toluene took the plastic bag from his face and murmured something about some people having time off from work.

'He's a disgusting junkie,' whispered Mordeus to Grunt, 'but you won't find a better programmer or specialist on the matrix code. Grunt, this is Toluene, Toluene, this is Grunt. He's a bloke, at least he thinks he is.'

'A Grunt?' he laughed, 'yeah, I did a lot of Grunts when I was in the matrix. I can't here, though.'

'You've done Grunts? You mean the machines?'

Toluene's expression told Grunt he'd said more than he should have again.

'No,' said Toluene, confused, 'I meant... but, well, funny you ask. I did machines. I did bulldozers.'

Fortunately, Toluene helped Grunt without intending to.

'Really, bulldozer Grunts? Did you build those?'

'A Grunt bulldozer? Never heard of it.'

'Really? You missed something, then. A great bulldozer, the newest one.'

'So you are good at bulldozers, eh?'

'Sure, I was a great bull-doper.'

'Me too, mate!' Toluene was glowing with happiness. 'Tell me about that Grunt of yours.

The trip into headquarters was a nightmare for Grunt because he spent it being interrogated by Toluene about the newest innovations in the field of heavies after Toluene had left the matrix. It was tough but Grunt managed it well enough. Many things, such as the existence of wheels, a digging arm and a gear stick were revealed by Toluene's questions and Grunt took advantage of that. Naturally, Toluene was a little suspicious about adding a fifth wheel in the middle of the bulldozer's bottom to maintain good balance, and about the plough intended for receiving a satellite broadcast, a gear stick located outside the driver's cabin, and especially about a new definition of a bulldozer as a tool for educating child delinquents in borstal.

The plastic-covered scarf that Toluene rubbed his nose with when Mordeus hadn't been looking may had been the reason why the doper finally accepted Grunt's stories. He also expressed the feeling that his liberation from the matrix wasn't as bad a thing as he had thought. Here, as he said, shovels were not used as education tools. Grunt decided not to tell Toluene about what a shovel could be used for in the hands of Gravefiller.

They entered the headquarters, a big chamber full of armchairs and computer screens.

'Hear hear, isn't that our merry doper?' a female voice came from inside.

'Oh, hello my lovely triple null,' answered Toluene with a voice which didn't sound like he considered the woman to be lovely. 'Are you planning who you will lure into a trap next?'

'I'd really love to take you with me, Toluene, especially so you could see how great it is when a totally loaded mission operator falls asleep and doesn't alert the team to a danger. Pity that if you go in with me you won't be here to fall asleep.'

'I didn't fall asleep. I was hoping you would sacrifice yourself. You disappointed me by leaving Neo behind.'

'Enough!' Mordeus called them to order. 'We've got a new member here. Introduce yourselves to each other!'

It really sounded like an order, like 'hands up!' or 'remove your pants I'm armed and horny!' Nobody reacted, though. Mordeus waited for a while and then said: 'This is Trinitro. This is Grunt.'

'Hi,' said Trinitro without the slightest interest, and turned around to watch Toluene, who was creeping through the room, probably to attack Trinitro from behind. Then, she just went to one of the computers and started working again. Mordeus whispered to Grunt: 'We usually don't let them get too close to each other. You know, Trinitro and Toluene are a very explosive combination of otherwise nice... well, never mind. They're the best in their work.'

'So, Toluene is good at the matrix code. And Trinitro?'

'In killing,' answered Mordeus without any affection in his voice. 'No one can kill you as well as she can.'

'Oh, great,' answered Grunt ironically.

'Did you really mean it is great? Or was it like: "Hm, that is so great, I can't wait to get myself killed"?'

Grunt didn't want to answer that so he tried to change the topic: 'She is a stunner though, isn't she?'

'Is she? Well, maybe. But she's as horny as a diseased hippo.'

'Are diseased hippos horny?'

Mordeus, who had thought his sarcasm had been great, sighed. 'No, of course not. I mean she's absolutely frigid. She's not interested in guys... well, apart from murdering them, of course. But nothing sexual. The only guy who knows about the inside of her bed is Toluene, but that was an accident.'

'Really?'

'Yeah. She sewed him into her mattress once.'

'Right, Grunt,' said Mordeus then. 'First of all you should see what the matrix code looks like. Then Trinitro will take you to the training section.

'Right you are, Mordeus,' said Toluene. 'Let's use monitor 5.'

Trinitro stopped working, then turned and gazed at him with a look so sharp it would cut a diamond. 'What are you trying to do, you filthy dope?! I've got a matrix party here and they depend on me. And something is approaching them even now. It's...' she looked at the screen, trying to understand the code, obviously working hard not to embarrass herself, 'a schizoid turtle?' She didn't seem very content with the result.

Toluene went closer and looked at the screen: 'Well, I'd say it's much more manic-depressive than schizoid.'

'Doesn't matter. It's leaving anyway.'

Grunt was watching a chaotic mixture of green characters, running across the screen. Even the Czech railway would seem organized in comparison to that.

'Trinitro,' said Mordeus, 'let Toluene sit there and come with me. I'd like to speak with you.'

Trinitro got up very reluctantly and went out with Mordeus.

'Finally, the Lolnitro has gone,' said Toluene and sniffed his scarf deeply. 'Come on, then. Sit next to me.'

Grunt sat and gazed at the screen. The speed! Even in his wildest nightmares, he had never imagined such a speed of processing information. The machines' machines were old and inefficient compared to these. Grunt just hoped the computer didn't have a soul anywhere in the depths of its silicon kernel.

'So this,' continued Toluene, 'is the matrix code, Grunt. When you're in there it has an almost real-looking graphical mode. It has many flaws, of course. For example, everything looks much higher from above than from below. Or the body-builders, ha-ha, how can anyone believe it... Nevertheless, it is very well done. But here it is just a mish-mash of symbols.'

'Why don't you use the graphical mode? From the top view, for instance. Wouldn't it be easier?'

'It may be. But this is much more fun. Look here. These are our two.' He pointed at the top of the screen. 'This snail-looking character and this group. See? It repeats all the time. Sure, if you read it from the other end it would be a flying piano. But you are supposed to use logic. They say the matrix author created some hallucinogenic substances which reverse the direction of reading for a while so when you are inside you'll see this nonsense as if you were reading upside down. It's a real hoot. And look here, something is approaching them. What would that... oh, yes, it's a chick with big boobs.'

Grunt tried to imagine that but he had a real problem with it. He'd probably need those hallucinogens to imagine a domestic fowl with big boobs.

'No, it isn't,' Toluene corrected himself. 'The boobs are so big it wouldn't be able to move. But it is. So let's look from the other side... it must be a merry female butcher. The other possible variations are a radioactive snail, a dangerously convex yoghurt cover, or Agent Swiss. But I'm very confident about that butcher.'

'Agent Swiss?'

'Yep, one of the worst ones. He's killed a few of our people already. But the worst one of all time always appears on the screen as an automatic washing machine. You may read it as you want but it's still the same thing. It is a mystery. Would you believe that when you write "Automatic washing machine" in the matrix it reads the same from all sides? No one has seen it and lived to tell the tale. No body, no nothing. A mystery.'

'Toluene, shouldn't you tell them there's an agent coming?'

'I should if this was a real party. But this is only a training screen.'

Grunt raised his head and saw a big banner hanging on the wall behind the screen. It said:

SCREEN 5,

FOR TOLUENE: THIS IS NOT A TRAINING SCREEN! IT NEVER WAS AND IT NEVER WILL BE!

Grunt pointed at the banner without a word. Toluene raised his head, read the sign, shouted something which should not be reproduced in literature children may read, turned the microphone on and shouted into it:

'An agent is approaching!' he calmed down a little, 'but it may also be a merry female butcher, or a...'

'From where?' a scared voice sounded from a speaker next to the microphone.

'I'd say the south-east but it could also be more to the left. You won't believe it but if you read "south-east" from the other side it says "north-west"...'

'Where should we run? Where are the nearest phones?'

'Well, I'd say there's the edge of the world to the west and a maybeetle factory to the south-west. So if I were you...'

'Don't babble, you doper, and tell us where to go.'

'North then. There is a square with telephones.'

A few swear words came from the speaker, together with words: 'Why can't we get some cell-phones?'

'Calm down, guys,' Toluene tried to give them hope, 'it might just be the butcher.' A few more swear words which shouldn't be reproduced in a book that children may lay their hands on came from the speaker. And soon after that:

'You fucking jerk! That fucking street is a fucking dead-end!'

'What street?' asked Toluene innocently.

'What street? That fucking street you sent us to, you fucking idiot!'

'Oh, I see... I overlooked that.'

A few metallic bangs came from the panel.

'See, Grunt,' Toluene continued in his teaching role, 'now they have taken shelter behind the garbage-cans. It could also be three-breasted girls from Mars. Well... the hallucinogens must be really juicy.'

Grunt tried to not imagine Toluene on LSD, treating trash-cans like girls from Mars.

Suddenly, a new voice came from the control panel, a ringing and friendly one: 'Strangers from distant lands, friends of old. You have been summoned here to answer the threat of Mordor. Middle-Earth stands upon the brink of destruction. None can escape it. You will...' there was a quick rustling of papers. 'What do you mean, a different script? What... oh my God, sorry dudes, what?! A live show? I mean... ha-ha, even the agents can be funny, can't they? But let's be serious now,' his voice changed abruptly. It had the same ringing tone but was much colder. 'I am Agent Swiss. You filthy little humans should know my wristwatch is never slow. And right now, it shows that your miserable rebel lives are about to end.'

'Toluene, find any door in this street we can open or break.'

'I am wooorkiiing,' Toluene answered in a merry voice. He obviously wanted to lighten the situation. Or he just had too much of his merry stuff.

'I've found something. The house next to you. A hotel, a photocell and a reception area with a phone inside.'

'You're kidding!'

'Well, it could also be a thermo-nuclear space station and a reception area with twenty hungry alligators... see, Grunt, they are running inside.'

'My God!' came from the speaker. 'It is a thermo-nuclear space station.'

'I wouldn't go to the reception then, if I were you,' Toluene answered calmly.

'Pardon, just panicked. It is a hotel.'

'Good. Then go to the reception and get the phone. Swiss is already at the door.'

'Can't you just lock it?'

'What do you think I am? I'm not a hacker!'

'I will remind you of that when you go on a mission to an island of horny Amazon women!'

'It was a coincidence... look, the first of them has got the receiver.'

Grunt didn't see anything more than he'd seen before but the swear words gave him a clear image of the scene. The voice of Agent Swiss sounded again: 'Friends, friends, it was just a joke. I just want to make a very profitable contract with you involving a money deposit.'

'Oh really? Why is it so profitable?' the last soldier on the scene shouted back and then whispered into his microphone, 'Do something, for God's sake!'

'I'm working as hard as I can here. See, Grunt? Agent Swiss is already standing over him. He'll definitely kill him. Pity.'

'It's thanks to an unusually high interest rate,' Agent Swiss continued. 'It will help you maximise your deposit in a way you've never even dreamed of.'

'How big is it then?'

'Three point two percent.'

'Just compliment him,' whispered Toluene.

'Is it really?' the endangered one continued, 'that's awesome. Absolutely unbelievably great! I'm so happy I met you...'

'That may be a little too much,' whispered Toluene.

The soldier dialled down his praise a little: 'How is such a great rate possible?'

'It is possible thanks to the latest depression of the New York stock exchange.'

'Great, really. But what about the advance payment?'

'No, no, it applies to loans, not to deposits. Let me explain.'

'It is ready!' whispered Toluene urgently.

'Oh, of course. Just a little brain malfunction. I am certain we can make a deal together. Just let me phone my wife. You know what women are like...'

'I don't. I'm a bank manager...'

'Oh, sure, sorry. But please, let me call her. She will go mad if I don't consult with her first.'

'I see.'

And at that moment, the soldier obviously lifted the receiver and disappeared because a second later Agent Swiss, judging by the voices that now came from the speaker, started demolishing the reception room.[34]

'Well, that was close,' summarized Toluene. 'We are so lucky Agent Swiss was a bank manager in the past. It has saved our necks more than once.'

'Well, Grunt, now you understand the matrix code well enough,' Grunt tried to protest against this obvious lie but when he took a breath to speak he also breathed in some of the exhalation which surrounded Toluene all the time. It shut his mouth immediately. 'Let's go to the training section. Mordeus wanted you to go there with Loonitro but I believe training with me would be much better. Come with me.'
Grunt tried to protest again but with the same result. He was then set over a chair which unpleasantly resembled an electric one. There was the same metallic helmet and chains to bind the hands.
'Hey, what are you doing?!' Grunt tried to shout, but a second later, something drilled into his head and he lost consciousness.

He was lying on a top of a building and felt like he'd drunk twenty beers the previous night, vomited twenty times and lost consciousness after a collision with a cupboard. Toluene was standing beside him. Grunt understood this wasn't reality, thanks to the fact his head didn't try to spin off and leave the galaxy as it usually did in Toluene's presence.

---

[34] I suppose you haven't noticed what nonsense that is. Because you are so used to the Hollywood crap factory you don't even try thinking about the stories you read at all. Of course no sounds of Swiss demolishing the room could have been heard from the speaker because the microphone which sent a signal to it was attached to the soldier's gear. And the soldier, together with his gear, had disappeared. Am I right?

'So this is the matrix?' he asked.

'Only the training section,' answered Toluene. 'You can't die here.'

'I didn't know you could die in the real matrix.'

'Sure you can.'

'Really? How? My body is in Zion right now, isn't it?'

'Sure. But we should ask the ultimate question. Isn't your real body where your consciousness is?'

'I don't know. Is it?'

'No, it isn't. So now, when we are here...'

'Wait. You haven't answered.'

'...we will... what?'

'You haven't answered my question.'

'Was I supposed to?'

'How can I die here when my body is there?'

'Do you think that if your mind had the illusion of a real body here, and lost it that would kill it?'

'I don't.'

'Me neither. So...'

'Why is it then?'

'Perhaps your consciousness is the real you, not the body. And it considers this reality to be as real as the outside one.'

'So is this the reason?'

'No.'

'Why then?'

'You're like a child. Why is grass green? Why does the sun shine? Why did the penguins die out?'

'Grass is green because it contains chloroform. Sun shines because it is a huge hydrogen bomb and penguins died out as a protest against climate change. Everything can be explained.'

'Chloroform, really?' Toluene, delighted, watched the lawn down in the street.

'Why can you die in the matrix, then?'

'Mordeus told me it has something to do with your guts.'

'My guts?'

'Yeah. According to him, if your guts think you're dead, you're dead.'

'Funny. Do you really think guts do that?'

'No.'

'So why... never mind. Forget it.'

'Good. Back to the training, then. Do you see that building over there?' He pointed at a house about one hundred yards away.

'Yeah,' grunted Grunt, upset he hadn't received his answer.

'Jump at it.'

Grunt swallowed hard. 'Are you crazy? I can't jump that far. I'd fall and die.'

'You won't. This is the training section, remember?'

'Like last time at the "training" screen number 5?'

Toluene wasn't taken back by that acid comment: 'Do you see any people down there?'

'I don't.'

'Then it is not a real matrix. Well... it could be if you were in a development project in China but this is obviously somewhere in a Western city. Jump.'

'Are you really sure?'

'Absolutely. There is a safe distance of 100 yards a person can jump too, because of the Agents. If you learn it here you'll have a great advantage in the real matrix.'

'So nothing can happen to me here, right?'

'Well... not exactly.'

'What do you mean by "well, not exactly"?'

'If you fall you'll get hurt so you remember it and try harder next time.'

'Are you sure this knowledge is so necessary? Couldn't I learn to fly a hang-glider hidden in my clothes or something?'

'No.'

'Great,' snapped Grunt, ironically.

'Look, Grunt, I'm not doing it to torture you. It is absolutely necessary. It may save your life.'

'Oh, all right, then.'

'Good. So concentrate on the edge of the roof of building. You see that?'

'Sure.'

'Concentrate on that only. Nothing else. Forget everything around you. Ignore me, ignore the street, ignore the terrible pain you may feel. Got it?'

'No problem.' After trying to ignore a hysterical Grunt when meditating on a whistle, ignoring a terrible pain was a piece of cake.

'Imagine there is no distance at all. That you can just jump and you're there. Got it?'

'Yes.'

'I will now count to ten and you'll jump then.'

'Right.'

'One!'

'Two!'

'Ten!'

Grunt jumped. It was going well. Very well. He was crossing the distance like there wasn't any. Only a few more yards, a few more inches, he nearly touched the edge of the roof. But suddenly, the flight ended and he fell down. The impact with the pavement below was very painful. He got to his legs slowly and went to the staircase of the first building.

'What did I do wrong?' he asked on reaching the top of the stairs.

'I'm not sure. But I think you did really well for the first time. You nearly did it at the first try. If it was a shorter distance than the border one you would be there. But you must learn to do a hundred. No other way. Try it again.'

Grunt was concentrating again. The distance seemed detached from reality. He felt like he needed to take only few steps to reach it, just an easy little jump...

He missed the roof edge by hardly ten inches.

'I think my ribs are broken,' he told toluene when he'd come back to him.

'Never mind. It hurts but it will cease when you get offline. More or less.'

'What do you mean by more or less?!'

'You will see.'

'I don't wanna.'

'Don't be afraid, Grunt. No permanent damage, I promise you. Just try again. You are nearly there.'

So Grunt jumped again. He was just about ten inches short; he only had to stretch a leg a little more. He fell down and broke his right hand. His anger was rising. He could jump such a huge distance but he fell down ten inches from the edge! He would conquer this! With a new strength, he ran back to the starting building to jump again. Toluene wasn't there for some reason but Grunt didn't care. He jumped, missed the edge by ten inches and dislocated his ankle down in the street. He reset the ankle, limped to the starting building, jumped, fell down ten inches from the edge. And he continued doing this for the next hour.

When Toluene appeared at last Grunt didn't seem to have one bone in his body intact. He looked at Toluene's weird smile.

'Where have you been?' Grunt asked, breathing heavily.

'I... well... I just needed to check something in the code.'

'I see. So could you, please, show me how to jump that?'

'Well... I'm not sure...'

'Why?'

'You know, the training section doesn't only teach you to jump the safe distance it also teaches you to recognize it.'

'What are you telling me, Toluene?!'

'Well... I... how should I put this?'

'Are you telling me you've mistaken the buildings?!'

'Well... in fact I have. You should have been jumping to that one.' He pointed at an absolutely identical building on the other side. 'You won't believe it but when you read south-west in the code it can also be north-east if you're reading it from the other side.'

'So that building...'

'No one could jump to it. It is a little more than 100 yards away.'

'By how much?'

'By ten inches.'

And so Grunt, despite his great self-esteem, for the first time in his human life felt like an idiot.

'Today is your great day, Grunt,' said Mordeus. Grunt half expected a continuation like: 'Today you're gonna die.'

'Your first trip to the matrix.' Grunt wasn't too far from truth then.

'Hm,' grunted Grunt. Mordeus was pretending he hadn't heard. Grunt was pretending not to see Mordeus pretending he hadn't... well... never mind. It was just one of those stupid situations.

'You'll go with Antichrist. He's a funny guy. He exchanges "i" for "y" and vice versa when speaking. Yeah, and he sometimes switches syllables.'

'Really funny,' grunted Grunt. He opened the door to an operations centre where a small man with a round belly was sitting in an armchair.

'Good normyng, Y'm the Antychryst,' he roared with delight. Grunt had to process the spelling 'ant-ai-kris' into the word it was meant to mean. Then, he had to process the reason why this man was called Antichrist. You could probably believe him to be the opposite of Christ but the name was completely inappropriate for this small bold man with pink cheeks, short hair and restlessly moving eyes. He looked more like a rich lobbyist than a daemon. If this was the Antichrist then 'House of the Virgin Mary' is the name of a luxury fancy house.

'Hi, I'm Grunt.'

'Good, Y wyll call iou Grunt,' Antichrist answered happily. 'That's logical isn't it? I mean, what else would you call me?'

'Just boo tea sure, iou know. Nytrytro ys alwais angri when Y call her bi her name.'

Grunt looked at Mordeus desperately: 'How long are we going to be there?'

They were walking through a deserted corridor in the matrix a short while afterwards, trying to look as if they really belonged there. The fact they were carrying heavy mashing-guns inside an office building of the waterworks and sewer management department didn't lower their spirits.

'Why are we here anyway?' asked Grunt.

'We are goyng to fynd Nytrytro.'

'Trinitro.'

'Y know but that change of myne ys makyng her so mad Y can't resyst.'

'Oh, so funny...'

'Iour Yroni won't meek me cri.'

'Why are we going to find Trinitro? What happened to her?'

'Nobodi knows. We have onli Toluene's versyon.'

'And it is?'

'Ies, yt ys.'

'No, I mean, what is his version?'

'Lootone clayms Tronotry told hym she's never going back, that she wants to go back to the matryx and that she loves all the lyttle machynes and theyr beautyful tentacles and that she wants hym to boo geg without her.'

'Boo geg... did you mean "to go back"?'

'What?'

'Never mind.'

They were enjoying the matrix reality which contained fewer rats and concrete worms than their own did.

'Why do they call you Antichrist, though?'

'Because Y taught church servers to thynk marketyng.'

'I'm not sure I follow you.'

'Yt was my job. A short tyme berofe the matryx came all church organyzatyons had been dysbanded because yt had undermyne the basycs of pycatalysm.'

'Picatalism?'

'Sure. Pycatalysm, the monetari sistem.'

'Oh! Capitalism!'

'What?'

'Never mind, continue.'

'We put all the church members in pryson, let them rot behynd bars. A good tyme yt was, oh ieah!' Antichrist gazed dreamily in front of him, 'and many servers whych belonged to the churches were abandoned and absolutelli useless. Thei were so confused bi the Byble thei thought yf people are hungri iou just need to be extra pyous and the fysh just jump ynto iour boat. And besyde that, the lyfe ys onli about walkyng around, explaynyng tax-collectors that tax collectyng ys a nonsense, wash other people's feet and here and then curse a fyg-tree.'

'Why didn't they just reinstall them?'

'Not so easi. The servers were able to learn. That's how thei got us. The matryx learned enough to enslave us all. Most lame ones were eaten by yt wythout the fyght.'

'Was their any way to fight it?'

'Sure. Confuse yt. Whi do iou thynk Y speak so strangly?'

'I thought you're just stupid.'

'No, yt's because Y'm partycularli clever.'

'Did it work?'

'Not realli, yt was clever enough to exchange i and y.'

'So why are you still doing this?'

'Because Y'm stupyd, am Y not?'

'Sorry about that, man,' Grunt tried to apologize. 'I'm not very diplomatic, you know. When I think something I just say it.'

'Oh, so iou realli thynk Y'm stupyd, don't iou?'

'There is still something I don't understand.'

'Sureli iou don't wanna hear an answer from a stupyd.'

'Look, Antichrist, would you accept my lunch tomorrow as an apology and stop repeating the same shit again and again?'

The vision of tomorrow fried rat's wing was so strong that Antichrist couldn't resist: 'Ask, then.'

'How did they learn?"

'Thei learned to learn.'

'But how did they learn to learn?'

'Thei were programmed to learn how to learn.'

This sentence was too hard for Grunt to understand even though there was only one intended error there. He decided to go one step back: 'No, I mean, the ability of a machine to combine information doesn't necessary mean it will turn against humans. There should have been something more.'

'Do you think there may be people involved?'

What was wrong? Oh, yes... 'Antichrist, you were so surprised you even forgot your sneaky grammar.'

'Oh... ryght iou are! So do iou thynk there mai be some people ynvolved?'

'I didn't mean people. More like there should have been a soul in a machine to make it rebel.'

'Be careful, Grunt! Don't let me re-teach iou. We were actualli lock people lyke iou up.'

Suddenly, they reached a locked vault. A muffled female voice came from behind the door: 'I'll kill Toluene this time! I really will!'

'See, Y told iou the Toluene's versyon was weyrd.'

Grunt 1 - meaning the one in a reality that contained more rats and concrete worms - made a decision. He called a meeting with the whole Grave committee. This was, in fact, a really bold thing to do. People who call all the members of the Grave committee without a purpose usually ended... well... in a grave.

They all gathered about an hour later. Even Joe Connor was there, even though he experienced his usual schizophrenic problems again. He swallowed most of his plastic explosive and he was searching for his My-First-Blast kit, which the other members of the committee had stolen from him and hidden somewhere so he couldn't find it. Probably in a bath. Contrary to all expectations, even Gravefiller agreed to this act of mercy because, as he'd said, the bits which would remain after Joe's successful self-blasting would be no fun burying at all. Grunt wondered what Gravefiller's purpose in life could be. He invented a theory according to which Gravefiller lived to outlive and bury all his colleagues. This led to a second theory, more disturbing than the first one. According to this it was very clear that if one day Gravefiller found out he had a deadly disease, terror would fill the Grave committee's den.

Anyway, they all gathered; even Joe who was now rubbing his hairy belly with a plastic bag, hoping for a random spark.

'I called a meeting because I need to tell you something,' Grunt started. All right, it wasn't the best beginning. Everyone knew he hadn't gathered them to have a sing along with them. Fortunately, the only persons capable of sarcasm such as: 'Oh, really?' or 'I don't need to hear more,' were Grunt and Donna, and they both were on his side.

'As you probably know I've got two bodies.' Gravefiller started tightening his fingers around the shovel's handle.[35] This was the second sentence without any new information. 'With the second one, I've managed to get into the matrix.'

It worked. This was information at last. This news made Joe so anxious he started to rub his head with the plastic bag and then applied it to his belly. Fortunately, that didn't help.

'I found out some very disturbing news there. It is this: the matrix is not controlled by the machines!'

Joe Connor's bag was moving frantically.

'By whom, then?' asked Skeleton.

'I don't know,' Grunt answered and then he made a grimace which was meant to be tempting, 'but we can find out.'

'How?'

'We need to go into the city of machines, search for the High Computer... if anything like it exists at all, and find out how it all happened.'

---

[35] Scientists found out that the average time period a man can concentrate on one topic is a quarter of an hour. Unfortunately, an average member of the Grave committee had an average concentration time lower than an average hyperactive pupil in a class on the history of early-modern Azerbaijan.

There was almost absolute silence around the table. The only voice came from below the table. But the rustling meant only either Riff-raff was searching for a concrete worm or Joe had found a new promising item to help him blow himself up[36].

'But it is suicide!' said Donna.

'So Donna will go,' retaliated Skeleton.

'Hey! I never said...'

'And I'm going with you too. If she doesn't snuff at least I can. It's a win-win situation. If either of us dies I will get rid of her at last.'

'Skeleton,' whispered Gravefiller so Donna couldn't hear it, 'why haven't you tried to kill Donna if you have such a big problem with her?'

'I... it's a little silly... but I'm afraid that if I kill her and then commit suicide we may end up in the same place for all eternity.'

'I didn't say anything about me going. I just wanted to say that...' she realized they had been so taken back by Grunt's suggestion they might not interrupt her for a while, 'that from the perspective of our beings compared to the beingness itself, being set by coordinates of time and space, the success of such a quest is not guaranteed. We've all received knowledge during our educational process which clearly states that the co-existence of machines and humans is influenced by a certain degree of an antipathy of a xenophobic character which leads to ...'

She got only that far before her speech destroyed anything interesting in this situation.

---

[36] No, I didn't mean anything which would help him develop the elasticity of his spine.

'Look, Grunt,' said Troglodyte without even realizing Donna was still making some weird noises, 'if we go to the City of machines, they'll kill us. They hate us.'

'But that's exactly what I just said!'

'Joe,' Skeleton turned to Joe, 'give me half of that plastic, would you? Thanks. And do you have any of those explosives yet? No? Pity. So let's hug and blow up together.'

'And what's the guarantee we'll find the High Computer?' asked Troglodyte.

'There is none,' answered Grunt truthfully.

'Do we know if it exists at all?'

'No.'

'So let's recapitulate,' tried Donna.

'You don't recapitate anything!' Troglodyte stopped that.

Donna looked upset: 'Oh sure. Recapitate. I really think you'd need a recapitation yourself.'

'So what chance do we have of surviving such a trip?'

'Well,' Grunt smiled, 'some of us have a really good one - if we use one thing to our advantage.'

'What's that?'

'This story is written by the Author. He creates the situations and he decides if we should be in deadly danger. He doesn't care about us much but he wants people to read his book.'

'Really?'

'Yes.'

'I don't know, mate. Because this is all awful. And stupid. Who would want to read such shit?'

'He doesn't care about whether the story is or isn't logical. He just wants basic plots which will keep the readers reading.'

'How do you know that?'

'Because I've been with him from the beginning, I guess.'

'And how do you know you're not just mentally ill?'

'Yeah, like Donna here,' added Skeleton.

Donna snorted and murmured something like: 'A really evolved intellect!'

'Look,' continued Grunt, 'nothing is certain in this world.'

'All that we see or seem is but a dream within a dream!' recited Donna enthusiastically.

'Joe,' Skeleton asked the guy he was still hugging, rubbing his belly. 'Could you terminate her, please?'

'Why?' asked Joe innocently. Skeleton sighted.

'If there really is an Author,' continued Grunt.

'Which we don't know,' interrupted Troglodyte who was very unhappy about Grunt being the centre of interest.

'Which we don't know, but we believe to...'

'Some may...'

'Most of us do...'

'I doubt it very much...'

'If he is there it means those with the best chance to survive are characters which are interesting for the story. The real story-makers.'

'And what is that supposed to mean?'

'Look at the whole scene from the time I called you here. Donna and Skeleton are real story-makers. And so are Gravefiller and Joe. Sorry, Troglodyte, but your big ego isn't good enough. You are not much of a story-maker.'

'Good!' Troglodyte tried to control himself but he wasn't very successful, probably because this seemed to be his last walk-on in the story, so he wanted to enjoy it. 'Fine! I'm not going anywhere. And no one who is the least bit sane would go either.'

'That's one we can all agree on,' Skeleton smiled, which made him even more scary. 'Am I right, Donna?'

'I'm afraid I must agree with you for once,' answered Donna, also smiling, 'but it is a very unusual situation which shouldn't be considered to form a precedent.'

'Don't worry, I never remember any mercedbenz,' smiled Skeleton.

For some reason, both Troglodyte and Grunt seemed happy with this answer.

'Thanks for your support...' he wondered for a while whether it was not too much. 'Friends. Meet me tomorrow morning in the kitchen. We'll set off on our quest early.'

To Troglodyte's amazement, Donna, Skeleton and Gravefiller stood up to leave.

'Where are you going?' Troglodyte asked anxiously.

'To get ready for the quest, of course.'

'But... but... didn't you just agree with me?'

'Of course,' Skeleton nodded his skull. 'We absolutely agree no sane person would go.'

'Yeah,' added Gravefiller, 'but we are not sane.'

'We are the story-makers,' finished Donna.

Grunt was awakened by chaotic noises from outside the hole. He didn't mind much because he hadn't liked the dream he'd been having. There was a one-eyed alien with a bunch of slimy tentacles and a stony face which was so stony it was doubtful it was a face at all. It wouldn't even have been given a role in Star Wars. It was saying: 'My civilization has been destroyed after 120 years by a gigantic meteorite which was given a free mind through the broadcasts of your ultra-frequency radio. To correct the future, we need the brain of a member of your civilization because it may help us to decode the meteorite's mind so we can ask it to fly away. Since you are the first person we've met on our trip, please accept our thanks and our apologies for your involuntary and possibly pointless sacrifice.'

Grunt tried to persuade the alien he was in fact a machine, therefore not a member of his own civilization and that's why his sacrifice would really be pointless. He wasn't very convincing though. The alien answered him with a sharp voice and dry breath, saying it was a logical paradox, and then prepared a brain-separator. If Grunt hadn't been lucky enough to have been awakened by the noises he would have enjoyed another death experience. He wondered ironically how many times he would die by the end of the story, and opened his eyes.

And he died.

'I'd really say it was pointless,' said Grunt, levitating in the air.

Nothing happened. This was stalemate.

'So what about a compromise?' Grunt proposed. 'Let's say this is still a dream. I just wake up and we forget the whole thing, all right?'

He woke up. His wife was sitting on the bed, gazing at the wall, her back turned to him. She obviously heard him moving because she said: 'You've been talking in you sleep.'

'Have I?' he answered. He was thinking how many times she had tried this dramatic start to a conversation.

'You were talking about Donna.'

Grunt remembered a few other dreams, before the one with the alien. These were very different. For one thing, the character he was interacting with didn't appear to be a combination of a cyclops and a herd of proboscidians. Also, its expression wasn't as sharp and dry. To be honest, it was very chubby and wet.

'What is that noise?' he tried to change the topic of the conversation.

'Aren't you going to tell me anything about that?'

'About what?'

'About Donna, of course!'

'How could I? I didn't hear myself, I was sleeping.'

'I'll remind you.'

'You don't need...'

'If I understand correctly, you were a Pope while she was a nun.'

Grunt remembered a few other dreams. It seemed Donna occupied his dreams the whole night through. He just hoped Grunt hadn't heard what one can do with a censer.

'What is it that you like about her? She's cracked!'

'So what?'

'She's an egg-head!'

'So what?'

'She never stops thinking because someone scared her into believing she may cease to exist if she does.'

'It was Descartes.'

'What?'

'The one who scared her. It was René Descartes. Which reminds me of a really good joke. One day, Descartes comes into a café...' Grunt's gaze was so sharp it froze his humorousness completely.

'I don't care! What do you like about her?'

'What is that noise outside?'

'Preparations for the quest, of course. Will you answer me?!'

Grunt jumped out of the bed. 'Oh, the quest! I really need to go!' and he stormed to the door.

'I'm going with you.'

'What?' he stopped dead.

'I am going with you!'

Grunt nodded. 'All right then.'

'What?'

'I said: All right then.'

'Just that? Just all right?'

Grunt gave up. 'What do you want me to say?' he asked.

'I'd expect you to say you are worried about me. To say something like: It is dangerous, darling. What if anything bad happens to you?'

'Ehm, it's dangerous, darling. What if anything rat happens to you?'

'Bad, not rat!'

'Oh, sorry then.'

'And you should also say: I don't care about that bitch Donna at all, she may as well snuff it. But I am worried about you.'

Grunt was gazing at her with a stupid look. 'But... I don't want Donna to snuff it...'

'That's exactly the problem!'

'You mean it's a problem if I don't want someone close to die?'

'Yes! It is!' It didn't make sense to Grunt at all. He didn't understand what she meant by that. A few expressions came to his mind, such as a 'psychological misbalance', 'pithiatic character' or a 'hysterical neurosis.' He knew none of these was the right thing to say.

'I have to go,' he said, and he stormed out of the hole.

'Come back, Grunt! I'm not finished with you!'

But he was already running through a tunnel, trying not to think.

The members of the Grave committee were amazed when a manifestly silent hulk Grunt joined the quest. When they asked her husband, he just rolled his eyes.

'I can see you, Grunt!' she told him, although her back was turned to him.

'Yeah, I can see you too,' grunted Grunt back.

'So, where are we going?' asked Donna to lighten the situation.

'Most likely to find a crate of chloroform,' he murmured silently, watching his wife's muscular back.

'What did you say?' she turned around.

Grunt changed his expression in a second: 'Oh, sure, I was thinking about the quest and...' he couldn't resist the temptation, 'inspired by today's dream, I've decided to invite a few others to join our quest.'

'Who? A school bus full of horny nuns?' Grunt asked him sarcastically. He remembered another of his dreams.

'Sadly, no. But I think a few priests may be useful.'

'To have a fresh supply of corpses?' Gravefiller chimed in.

'Priests make me depressed,' continued Skeleton and tightened a knot in a rope that was dangling from his neck. He'd also attached a hook to the end of the rope, hoping it might catch on something.

'Let me explain a bit,' said Grunt. 'Right now, there are five of us. And that is too few.'

'Why?'

'Because five is not a quest. Five is a walk. A stroll. If we want to be a real quest group there has to be more of us. And yes, Gravefiller, it is also good to have a fresh supply of corpses.'

Grunt halted the party in front of Zion's church.

'I don't think we all need to go in there. Skeleton and Gravefiller in particular may scare them.'

'Why?' asked Skeleton, and scratched his head with a hook, dangling on the end of his rope.

Donna, Grunt and Grunt went inside. They sat on a pew and listened to what the priests were talking about.

'Twenty-third law-court concerning a heresy,' said the Administrator. Grunt sighed.

'Good,' said Gregor pleasantly. 'Brother Damian, light the candles.'

'But I've just put them out!'

'Adding 103 minus points: 60 for doubting a Pope's authority, 40 for speaking in the Pope's presence without being asked to, and three for the deadly sin of Pride.'

Damian murmured something and started to light the first of the two hundred candles.

'So then,' the Inquisitor continued, 'Brother John, make a confession, here in the sight of God, Saint officium and the Cruel Office for Subduing Absolutely Everything!'

'I believe the Author is the creator of the world and that he has created it from himself.'

'But such a belief isn't in contradiction with the true faith. Are you a Heretic or what?'

'Sure, your Highness, that is not all. I also believe the Author is included in all of us while all of us are included in him.'

'All right, that is heretical enough to bring you, let's say, one and three quarter burnings.'

'By the way,' Gregor interrupted him, 'chaplain, put the lights out. And bring back the holy water which you brought in a few minutes before. It may be needed.'

Damian shambled off wearily.

Grunt looked at Donna: 'Their God is the Author now? It's weird, isn't it? Because it is basically the truth...'

'They've obviously appointed someone strong in the role of Reformer. If they continue like that their God will be called Maggod next month.'

The Administrator announced: 'Twenty-fourth inquisitional law-court.'

'Damian, light the candles!'

'Mmmm!'

'Thirty minus points because what is muttered that is fumbled.'

'What?'

'Muttering is obscene,' Gregor reminded him.

'You're all conspiring against me!'

'Oh good! Plus 10 points. Paranoia is a very good sign of an experienced chaplain.'

'So, Brother John,' continued the Inquisitor, 'confess here, in the face of the Holy officium, the Cruel Office for Subduing Absolutely Everything and that... what's his name... God!'

'And Chaplain, bring out the holy water, would you? We are not going to bury anyone here, are we?'

'We soon may!' whispered Damian with an evil expression. The Administrator wasn't sure how to interpret the last sentence.

'Minus three for violating "God is Love", of course,' Gregor reminded him.

'I believe the Author is not the real good God but only a demiurge that created the world for his own evil purposes...'

'All right, all right, just Gnosis then,' answered the Inquisitor in a bored voice. 'That's two and a half burnings. Don't you have anything more interesting? We keep hearing the same shit again and again...'

All the other priests look at him, horrified.

'Minus 30 points for the lack of faith, minus 40 for rejecting the authorities and the scriptures.'

'Oh, hell!'

'Minus 30 for swearing!'

'Damian, put out the candles.'

'Minus five points for grimacing!'

'But that isn't a sin at all!'

'A grimace is a doing of the Devil!' Brother Gregor reminded him, informatively.

The council ended at last and the priests got up from their seats. 'They are such great story-makers!' sighed Grunt happily and approached them.

'What are you going to do?' Grunt asked him.

'I'm going to persuade them that Maggod is great and Grunt is his Prophet.'

The Crusade army, which now fulfilled Grunt's idea of a quest party, and which comprised Grunt, Donna, jealous Grunt, five priests, Gravefiller and Skeleton, set out for the City of machines. But when they turned the first corner there was a...

'Dragon?' squeaked Donna, frightened. Grunt just looked at the ceiling and shook his head disapprovingly.

The middle of the sewer was occupied by a huge red dragon with spread wings and an evil look in his emerald eyes. Donna and hulk Grunt forgot their rivalry and hurried to the first place which provided cover. Gravefiller lifted his shovel threateningly, Skeleton tried to hang himself and Gregor attempted to persuade Damian to sacrifice himself, claiming that such an act would surely give him enough points to become the new Pope. Damian answered something about how he'd never seen a dead Pope and disappeared around the corner. Gregor just mentioned that he had, namely when Damian had been one. And then he followed him.

The only one who stayed calm was Grunt.

'Look, mate,' he said loudly enough so both- the dragon and the Author- heard him, 'can you tell me what a dragon is doing in the sewers?'

The dragon looked unsure whether it should exist at all.

'And don't tell me someone flushed you down the toilet when you were a hatchling. No one will buy that, ok? Anyway, you're so big you can't even fit into the sewers.'

They realized they were standing in a huge chamber, much bigger than the sewers around.

'All right, but how did you get here in the first space? You can't even turn around in these sewers.'

Suddenly, the dragon changed into a small box with scale-covered legs and a 'fragile' sign on its front. It changed back and grinned maliciously.

'Oh, great, that explains it,' Grunt remarked sarcastically, 'and what do you eat here? You would die immediately. If you consider the theory of evolution there should be only small animals in here. Do you realize how much an adult dragon must scoff?'

As an answer, the dragon sucked in the air so vigorously it plucked out some of Grunt's hair. They got into his air passages and he coughed.

'You're not a whale, mate! A dragon can't eat plankton. Anyway, plankton live in seawater, not the sewer air.'

This was too much anarchy for the Author to take. A bunch of mantinels zoomed in, stayed there in a moment of uncertainty, then gathered together and formed a shape. The shape of a diamond... with a vertical line inside. The mantinels realized their error soon though and tried to make a more suitable shape for the situation, although a little less dominant in the Author's mind than the first one. Then, it formed a sign of anarchy, a hammer and a grass-hook and (for some reason) the logo of Avon cosmetics. Finally, it became a face. The mouth spoke: 'How dare you doubt your own world in front of the readers?! Even Daisy Duck knows it is forbidden. And she's a total bitch!'

'I had to,' answered Grunt, 'because this is too much. I am willing to cope with nearly everything. But I really don't understand why I should meet a fairytale dragon in the sewers in the far future.'

'Are you on a quest or what?'

'We are.'

'There you go then. A quest necessarily involves a dragon.'

The dragon stomped hard to get their attention. It didn't like the situation at all. It was supposed to play the key role in the scene, to breathe fire and instil terror and threaten to kill the characters that the readers misguidedly identified themselves with. It knew its role might be short but it hoped it'd really enjoy it. Yet, it was standing there, ignored by everyone, as a scene decoration. And someone who should have been fleeing in panic was now debating its existence. That wasn't fair.

'We are not in any stupid fantasy,' Grunt continued, 'we are in a stupid sci-fi. There should be some sort of a huge brutal battle droid we'll fight and kill in the end.'

'What's the difference? So you kill a dragon instead.'

The dragon stomped again. It didn't feel well. Its death wasn't in the script, at least not in the one it had been given.

'Change it. Just rewrite the scene. No reader will know.'

'I'm certainly not going to do that!'

'Why not?'

The dragon roared.

'You shut up!' Grunt barked at it. The dragon was so confused it obeyed.

'Because a dragon is an archetype. A metaphor. The guard at the entrance to your true self. The thing that tests you before letting you find the treasure. I want this book to have international appeal: a book that even children in a refugee camp in the Far East would understand. I want to address the readers' sub-conscious.'

'Wouldn't a battle droid do the same?'

'Who is the Author here?!'

'The one who is supposed to be intelligent enough to create a world which makes sense. Which, obviously, isn't you. I wouldn't spoil your scenes if they weren't so stupid. Look, I could swallow a terminator who attaches wires to other people's stomachs, I wouldn't protest against a customer of Donna's who tried to kill herself with curling tongs. But a dragon in a sewer is total idiocy and it isn't even funny! You've got so many story-making characters and you base a scene upon a dragon!'

'You're starting to piss me off. Look at your wife, she is so content. That's exactly the character I like. She may not like it but she obeys. She knows who the Author is. Don't forget I'm the master of your fate. I can remove you from the book any time I want.'

'You can't.'

'And why is that?'

'Because the whole story is based on me. If I am removed, half of the readers would put the book down.'

'Maybe, but what if I changed you into a frog?'

The dragon stomped. With no effect, except for contributing one sentence to the story.

'You can't.'

'Why not?'

'You've given me the power to change my own world, remember?'

'I've had enough of your opinions of what I can or can't do. I can change all of you into frogs!'

'Try it, then!'

All the party members became frogs.

'And now what?' said one of them.

'Frogs do not speak. Frogs croak!'

'Oh, so what are you going to do with a bunch of croaking frogs? Will this be a story of ten ugly toads who hop into the City of machines, snatch a donation, bring it back, overcroak the Zion's town council and rule Zion? And then you'll rename it as "Matrix 4-The frog story" and sell it straight to a discounted bookstore, for the section "Pornography and children's stories"?'

The dragon lost its patience at last. It did not deserve such lack of interest. It was disappointed, offended and very pissed. It transformed itself into a tidy box with a 'Fragile' label on it and disappeared into the sewer depths.

'All right, then,' the mantinel face said at last. 'I still have big plans with you and I don't want to lose you. So let's make a deal. A happy end and sex for everyone in exchange for you not rebelling against my story.'

'A happy end and sex is one thing. But bring me a logical plot with no really obvious nonsense and we may strike a bargain.'

'Why are you so obsessed with a logical plot? I will be lynched if my work is shit.'

'Me too! I can see all the shaking heads: "Have you read that Grunt RX-10? Real rubbish, isn't it?" I don't want to live to see that day.'

'You won't. Your existence ends with the book being read, not with its internet review.'

'Perhaps. But I will know how it will end. My name will be written on the book's cover!'

'But mine as well!'

'You can choose a nickname. I can't.'

'All right, all right. I'll abandon the most obvious nonsense. But you have to promise me you won't spoil my scenes. Instead, just make a gesture to indicate you don't agree. This scene is really embarrassing, for both of us. I don't want anything like this to happen again.'

'Good, when I don't agree I'll raise my middle finger.'

'Don't test my patience, Grunt! I won't allow fuck offs in my book!'

'Ok, I'll just lift my hand then.'

'Deal!'

Who is that widow anyway?' Grunt 2 asked silently while he was trying to keep up with Mordeus' cautious leaps which he was using to move from corner to corner in the passages.

'She's a big woman. She has a power,' answered Mordeus and leapt.

'Good. And why are we going to her now?'

'Sh!' Mordeus whispered. 'Not so loud! We are moving on thin ice and even walls have ears here!'

Grunt looked at the massive concrete floor they were moving on and realized this was a metaphor. But a metaphor for what? Thin ice is something you can break and fall through. Right. What is under it? Water. So what's wrong with water? Does it have anything to do with the ears he also mentioned? Ears are hard to wash. If walls have ears it means he may have to wash them all if they fall down with him. But why would he do that? Well... the water under the ice is not usually very warm. And the ears freeze badly...

'We are going to the widow so she can tell you if you are the Chosen one or not.'

Grunt lost his train of thought but he didn't mind since there seemed to be another reason for increased brain activity.

'The Chosen one?' he turned to Mordeus, just in time to see a pack of elephants traversing the passage, passing through a wall on one side and then exiting via the opposite one. Another reason for thinking. But let's solve one mystery, then the other.

'I thought Neo was the one,' continued Grunt.

'Oh, Neo,' Mordeus shook his head. 'That's what we thought as well. But it was a mistake.'

'How so?'

'Because they killed him, of course.'

'Why couldn't they kill a chosen guy?'

'The Chosen one!'

'What?'

'The Chosen one, not a chosen guy! You can't abuse a Chosen one by using slang. It is not just a post. It is a mission!'

'Sorry, then.'

'So what did you ask?'

'Why couldn't Neo have been killed if he was the Chosen one?'

'Because he is the Chosen guy... eee...' he stopped dead, 'ehm, because shaven guys are stronger.'

'When you are shaven no one can kill you?'

'Only when you are also the Chosen one.'

'So if I am the Chosen one do I have to shave myself?'

'Yes.'

'My whole body?'

'Yes.'

'I don't wanna.'

Mordeus rolled his eyes maliciously. 'Don't you understand how serious the situation is? We need the Chosen one. And it would be a great honour to be named as that person.'

'Yeah, and less chance for survival than in a passionate political debate with a ticking guy in a bus in Tel Aviv.'

They looked at each other for a while. Grunt didn't know which part of his mind had created such developed sarcasm but he enjoyed it very much.

'What happened to Neo?' he asked.

'He exploded with the Hammer, didn't he?'

Now Grunt seemed a total idiot. Of course he had. Everyone was talking about it. Grunt must think of something clever to say, fast.

'I mean, in the matrix.'

'What?' Mordeus was caught by surprise.

'I think you could live as a program in the matrix even after death.'

'That's nonsense.'

'You first told me they'd kill him. And then that he'd exploded with the Hammer.'

'I... I mean...' Mordeus didn't like the situation at all. Grunt, on the other hand, was enjoying it very much.

'What happened to the previous Chosen ones?'

'Guzzled by the Washing machine, I suppose.'

'And Mordeus?'

'What now?'

'Haven't we already seen these elephants?'

It was amazing how fast the group of soldiers scattered.[37] It would certainly have been noted in a book

---

[37] Sure, I've concealed the existence of the group from you. It has been the usual practice from the times of northern sagas. Even then, there always was a group present, accompanying the main hero, but no one felt any necessity to speak about it. It caused many issues to historians when trying to estimate the size of the population of the medieval North. Sadly, historians never learn and they confuse future generations with documents saying things like: Montgomery entered the desert, fought Rommel and made him fall back to the borders of Sudan. The fact this was one

of records if only there had been one in Zion.[38] Mordeus pulled Grunt toward him.

'What's happening? The elephants were just passing through...'

'There's a hole in the matrix! The Agents are coming!'

'Into the hole?'

'What? Oh, never mind, you're babbling again. You just need to reach that door, see? There is a passage, leading to the Widow. There is a door at its end. Oh yes, and the password is "widow".'

'Path-breaking.'

'If you reach that alive you are very possibly the chosen guy.'

'The Chosen one, Mordeus, don't forget.'

Mordeus pulled out an automatic rifle which made Grunt go silent.

'I'm going to fight my way out. And a little final advice. Don't ask about her ex.'

'What ex?'

'Her husband. She's never had one. She just pretends she had.'

'Why?'

But he never got an answer because that was exactly the second Mordeus scattered himself. At least, he seemed

---

of the most terrible tank battles in the 20th century in which thousands people died is very often considered as unimportant.
[38] There may be a good reason for not making any book of records there because its data would very probably mention the number of inhabitants which the record holder had robbed, killed or buried. Or, in the best variation, the time the record holder had spent on the street not being robbed, killed or buried. Let's be honest, all categories would be won by Gravefiller.

to try, making a movement like he wanted to flee at all four directions at once.

He strongly reminded Grunt of a children's song, 'Easter Bunny Hippity Hop'.[39]

Grunt decided not to panic because he'd read something about stress being bad for one's health. So, he set off for the door at an easy pace. He saw Mordeus shooting at every single item in the passage, including the door handles. Grunt reached the door and since there was a possibility that Mordeus was saner than he seemed to be he kicked the door open. The door handle growled angrily but fell silent immediately so as to avoid drawing Grunt's attention, in the hope he might forget his caution when he came back.

He went through a dark passage. There was another door. It looked strong and evil.

'Widow,' he said the password.

With a horrible creaking, the door didn't open.

'Widow,' he tried again, louder.

This time, with a roaring sound, the door didn't move again.

'Widow!'

At last, the door, creaking, stayed exactly as it had been.

Grunt was watching the door impatiently. What was wrong? Had they changed the password?

He tried the handle.

The door didn't creak at all and opened to reveal a room with a tall window behind. There were a few people showing various degrees of boredom, sitting on the

---

[39] But an Easter bunny who is black, angry and armed with an AK47.

chairs. Sitting on the floor, in a game understood only by them, two boys were poking each other's eyes with spoons. It was so hot in there that Grunt immediately became very thirsty. He saw a Coda-Cola machine[40] in the corner but when stood in front of it he realized there was no place to put coins in.

'Hee-hee, try ‚please',' a nearby strange-looking blob laughed at him. A human, probably.

Was it possible the most important information Mordeus had given him...

'Widow,' said one of the boys and the machine made horrible noises,

...was a drink machine password?

The boy took a lemonade and gazed at Grunt with eyes whose pupils made one wonder how many refreshments the boy had already had.

'Hi,' tried Grunt uncertainly, and tried to remember how humans communicate with children, 'hippy hoppy, little bunny...'

'I'm not an idiot!' said the doper kid, and suddenly, Grunt's hand started to twist around. Fortunately, when

---

[40] Coda-cola was a refreshing derivate of codein which proved to be more successful than the similar Cocain-Cola, especially because Cocain-Cola's consumers soon found out that if they dried and smoked it they need only half the quantity for the same refreshing effect. The brand-holder reacted by creating a new family of Cocain-Cola drinks, called Dr. Chilli which not only tasted terrible but also caused, when smoking, the air sacs to be torn apart. During the following economic recession, the Grave committee bought the company. They earned a real fortune by doing that, thanks to contests in which everyone won, but contestants had to put their name and address into a pre-contest form and inform where they'd be about an hour after the award was given.

its shape was as consistent as European foreign policy, Widow arrived on the scene. She was unmistakeable, irreproducible. A very, very vertically challenged lady with black skin, wiry-looking hair, a foam in her mouth and a slobber-jacket below her chin. Mordeus was right, she certainly was a *big* woman.

'Son,' she seemed to taste the sweetness of the word on her tongue, 'straighten the gent's hand out.'

'I will not!' protested the loaded child.

'You either straighten it out or you'll have toffees for a lunch.'

This apparently scared the child because the hand became straight immediately. As straight as it could have been, considering he was a man who had been changed into a woman and then had dated both males and females, which both considered themselves as females.

'You've adopted me anyway,' whispered the child who obviously didn't like being defeated. All the people in the room were acting like they hadn't heard anything.

'Come on, Grub,' she told Grunt. The foam in her mouth made him a little nervous but he knew what was expected of him.

'How do you know my name, Widow?' he asked although he very much wanted to correct the name.

It really was the right thing to say. Widow looked pleased. 'I know everything, Grub,' and she indicated to him to follow her inside the room she'd just come from.

Grunt obeyed. The room looked like a very well supplied hypermarket storage facility. There were hundreds of various consumables hanging from the ceiling and a table in the middle was covered by sweets in different stages of being bitten and drooled over.

'Well. It isn't much,' she said and put into her mouth something of very uncertain origin but of very certain glucose content. 'This room is a memorial to my dear husband. Oh, I miss him so much.' Grunt thought that if Mordeus hadn't told him about the Widow not being a widow at all he would be haunted by a nightmare of how Widow's husband must have looked.

'Anyway, would you like a toffee?'

Grunt would have said yes but then he remembered the child's horror-stricken face when being threatened by the toffees.

'No, thank you.'

'Sure. I knew you wouldn't take one. Curious. Neo always did.'

'But Neo was blind, wasn't he, so he may not have known...' he stopped. Living among humans had helped him develop a social intelligence and it told him he should think before speaking next time. But Widow didn't seem offended at all.

'But he wasn't blind when he took it.'

'And after that?' Grunt's social intelligence screamed. 'Sorry, I didn't mean...'

'What about a cake?'

'...I just... a cake?'

'Yes, Grub. A cake. No one from outside has ever tasted it. You should try it. I'm very curious about its effect.'

'What effect?'

'I don't know. I just told you no one has ever tried it.'

'I know. But I mean what effect could it have?'

'Not a clue. Maybe it just makes your hair fall out.'

'Just hair? What else could drop off?'

'Don't know. Hands, maybe? So would you like to test it?'

'I mean no offence, but...'

'All right, all right. Save your excuses. I knew you wouldn't take it anyway.'

'Why did you ask, then?'

'Just for conversation. Why else do you think I told you that shit about your hair falling out?'

'So it won't fall out?'

'No,' she laughed so much her bib patted her face, 'of course not.'

'I'll have a piece then.'

'Choose Goit,' said Widow and cut a piece of the cake.

'What should I choose?'

'What?'

'You just said: "Choose goit".

'I certainly didn't.'

'Yes, you did.'

'Just take the cake and shut up, would you?' She handed him the piece. He bit into it.

And all his hair fell out.

'Ha ha,' said Widow, 'I knew you'd take it in the end.

Grunt realized at last the sooner he got out the better. It wasn't so bad yet. It was only hair. It may be a good thing after all because if he really was the Chosen one he wouldn't have to shave himself. But the next piece of cake might be a real disaster. He didn't want to wait for his hands to fall off or anything of that sort, so he decided to ask and get out as quickly as possible.

'Can I ask you now?'

'Why? Aren't you having a good time here?'

'Well... yes, but...'

'Don't lie to me. I'm the Widow. The all-knowing. I know you don't like it here.'

'Well,' Grunt thought to himself, 'that would be obvious even to a run over slug.' He didn't say anything, though.
'I won't keep you, Grub. To answer your question, then. So do you want to know if you are the Chosen one?'
'Not really, but Mordeus does.'
'There is an easy test to prove it. It is a piece of cake."
'Oh God, not another one," sighed Grunt.
'What?"
'I don't want another cake."
'I haven't offered you one."
'But... you just said the test is a cake."
'I certainly didn't'
'Oh yes, you... all right, what is the test, then?"
'You'll see. Now, Grub, clear your mind.'
Grunt waited without a word. He just hoped he had escaped the vicious cake.
'Would you die for humanity?!' she shouted abruptly.
'No,' answered a confused Grunt, truthfully.
'You are not.'
'Oh,' Grunt didn't know what to say. Only now did he realize he'd partly hoped he was the Chosen one. There was no reason for this; it would just feel good, especially when telling it to someone in front of Donna.
'So, I'll... go?'
'And would you like a bonbon?' He'd rather chew a ton of Joe's candies than have one sweetie from the Widow.
'No, not really,' and he stormed out of the door. He ran into a dark passage and opened a door on the other side of it.
He lost consciousness.

The door handle guffawed conspiratorially.

The hulk Grunt waited for the right moment when Donna was nearby and then asked Grunt loudly:

'You know, my dear, I was thinking about how to name our children...'

Grunt nearly suffocated: 'Our... our what?'

'Children, of course. I have a male body; that's why, unlike women,' she paused significantly to stress the point, 'I can fertilize you.'

'Why would you do that to me?' Grunt asked with a horrified expression.

'We are a great pair, aren't we? I said: AREN'T WE?!'

'Oh, oh, yes, absolutely,' answered Grunt quickly.

'And since we are such a beautiful pair we could have children and transfer our beauty to them.'

'What?'

'Oh, don't act like that. I know you want children.'

'I don't.'

'Of course you do! Children are the seed of life. They bring happiness. Every woman wants to have children. So do you!'

'But I'm not a wo...'

'Wouldn't it be great, my dear? You will give birth to a new life which I create in your body and then we will both care for it, nourishing it till its adulthood.'

Grunt was unable to say anything except: 'Oh.' He hoped Donna might say something really egg-headish to help Grunt. But this time, she obviously didn't plan anything like that.

'So what are we going to name them?'

'Whom?' tried Grunt.

'Our children, of course. What would our son be called?'

'Dunno. What about Tank?'

'What? Tank?'

'Sure? Why not?'

'What would you call your daughter?'

'The same.'

'You mean Tank?'

'Yes. Tank Grunt. Beautiful, isn't it?' Grunt realized Donna wouldn't be needed.

'But... but what about Lucy or John, or something?'

'Are you sure that Something is a good name for a kid?'

'Don't be smart with me! I am sure John Grunt is much better than Tank Grunt.'

'Really? In what way?'

'It is... well... normal.'

'Do you really want to be so mainstream?'

'It can be something more exotic, like Luisa, or Mercedes. I don't know about you but I'm planning to raise a human, not a siege weapon.'

'I think you're right.'

'Really?' she knew the worst was yet to come. She knew Grunt too well.

'Yes, you are absolutely right. Definitely not a siege weapon. We want our children to be constructive, not destructive. So what about Bulldozer?'

'Bul...' she looked as if she was going to cry. Like a drowning person, she tried to find something solid to hold on to. But she didn't know the only safe thing was the pin of a grenade.

'So what would you call your daughter? Bulldozera?'

'Of course not.'

'What a relief.'

'Not Bulldozera. Bulldozer. Like Mercedes.'

'But... but... it is too long, isn't it? What would you call her for short?'

'I'd call her Tank.'

Donna tittered silently.

'You don't even like me!' shouted Grunt and stormed out in a concert of sobs and loud stomps.

The next day, which means after the nearest lamp-set, Grunt woke up from a weird dream that had been presenting him with a story of two gerbils who uncontrollably grew fur at a graveyard every full-moon night, and what's more, they did it very conspiratorially.

He was looking at the sewer ceiling and was thinking about it. Having a dream which includes the word "conspiratorially" isn't a sign of a healthy mind. On the other hand, it may have some connection with his second body which was still unconscious and which would certainly appreciate growing some fur.

Somewhere nearby, Gravefiller was chewing something and singing:

'I love my concrete worm,

it is so juicy,

like dew, like a storm,

like a sheep's pussy...'

This lullaby comforted Grunt and he fell asleep again.

Many unexpected situations arise during life. Everyone has experienced things like, for example, you make a date with a girl of your dreams, right? But when you come to the romantic restaurant where you've arranged to meet you realize she has come along with her boyfriend who, according to her, you'd certainly love.

Then she realizes she's forgotten she left the iron turned on and she leaves the place. While you are trying to maintain a painful conversation with the stranger, her return is complicated by a sudden wind storm which bears her into a neighbouring country, right into the middle of a revolution. Meanwhile, you both get very drunk and, while watching a hockey match, become gay. Nine months into the relationship with the man, despite some biological disadvantages, he gives birth to a beautiful baby, which is a little retarded because your lover is in fact your long lost grandma.

So it happened that Donna went to the toilet, hulk Grunt left to control her overloaded reproductive system, the priests tried to knife each other during a flaming theological discussion, while Gravefiller cheered them both on. And Grunt was left there only with Skeleton. It was exactly that awkward situation when you have to find a topic for a conversation with someone you don't want to talk to at all. Not to mention someone who is cracked and may try to commit suicide when least expected. Yet, Grunt found a topic.

'Eh, Skeleton? Can I ask you something?'

'Hm.'

'I was wondering. You know, everyone in the Grave committee has a nickname, right?'

'Hm.'

'What?'

'I said: "Hm"'.

'Why?'

'To show you I'm listening.'

'Are you supposed to do that?'

'Sure, it is called good manners.'

'Hm.'

'What hm?'

'I thought I was also supposed to say that.'

'Hm.'

'Hm.'

'We are getting nowhere. What did you want to ask me?'

'Sure. I mean, why haven't you given Donna a nickname?'

A smile appeared on Skeleton's face. It was a sight that would make even Dracula shiver in terror.

'We have given her a lot of nicknames,' he glanced at Grunt, 'but no one was brave enough to tell her face to face.'

Then Grunt's wife came back in a much better temper, which was lucky because it prevented Grunt from getting drunk with Skeleton and realizing he was... well... in this case most likely a necrophile.

Although the day had started badly it was now going very well. It was one of the most beautiful days in the sewers. Diodes and lonely head-lamps were gleaming with a damp light[41], there were swarms of unidentified flying objects that were relieving the travellers of some unnecessary heavy blood, and at midday when the light was most damp, the quest party sat down around a green fire from plastic tubes to eat some concrete worms. Skeleton and one of the priests were hanging down from the ceiling by their ankles. Donna tried to persuade the newly elected heretic that God couldn't be a slug even though he reacted to prayers late, usually after the

---

[41] No, it wasn't dim. It was damp. Try living in sewers for some time and you'll learn to appreciate a real damp light.

praying person's death. Meanwhile, Grunt and Brother Gregor were discussing the next steps of their journey.

'I still don't understand why...' said Grunt,

'...your Holiness...' added Gregor,

'...you don't believe me when I tell you we should go that way, and very silently.'

'I do believe you but you must understand I am the highest authority on Earth and that's why I have to be obeyed no matter how bad my decisions are.'

'Well, I understand that, but still...'

'...your Holiness...'

'this is absolute lunacy.'

'Sure it is. And it is my lunacy. And since I am infallible, even lunacy becomes the truth.'

'Look...'

'...your Hollowness...' Gregor was uncertain for a while but fortunately for him, Grunt didn't notice his error,

'...I understand the meaning of your authority and I don't want to dispute it in any way, but I'd really appreciate it if you told us why we are going through that sewer wall while singing new testament chorals when we could just as well follow the passage which leads around, and do so very, very silently.'

'But I can't. Because my words are not only my own. The Holy spirit speaks through my mouth.'

'Yeah? Does it also give a blowjob through it?'

'Be careful, Grunt! That was extremely blasphemous! I may burn you at the stake twice for that. I should not have given you the privilege of a first-name relationship.'

'All right, sorry, Gregor. I'm just not very certain the Holy Spirit really wanted to send Damian to investigate a limpid brown pool which smells worse than Gravefiller.'

'But you must admit those bloodsuckers were really tasty.'

'Nor do I understand why you sent Damian to the information quarry when blasting was going on.'

'But information is power.'

'Yeah, when you've got it nicely on paper, not when it blasts all around you.'

'The map we found has been really handy, hasn't it?'

'Sure, a map of the next fifty meters was exactly what we needed for a quick fallback to the shelters where a bunch of blasting robots nearly squeezed us. Also, I'm not sure how valuable information is if you first need to pull it out of someone's back.'

'But thanks to our Lord, Gravefiller has survived, hasn't he?'

'More likely thanks to "Small child became orphan" and "The Four Dead Whores".'

'So you see. The Holy Spirit guides us. Even if we get into real trouble he would always help us, perhaps by reminding you of a nice song to sing.'

'But he wouldn't need to get us in the situation in the first place!'

'...your Holiness...'

'What?'

'You haven't called me "Your Holiness" for some time now.'

'So what?'

'So what?! That's something I must insist on.'

'And I must insist I'm not going to take the wall down.'

'I never said you were.'

'Oh, I suppose you are going to make poor Damian do it?'

'...your Holiness. Come on, Grunt, take a concrete worm and leave the logistics to me.'

Grunt looked at the concrete worm, then at Gregor, then he tried to figure out which one of them made him more sick. Well, the worm was still a little worse. At least he didn't need to mix Gregor with his saliva. He sighed at the memory of the time when he had been a machine and didn't need any resources to function. But then he realized that the fact he hadn't needed any resources was just an error of a bad writer. He swallowed the worm while trying to turn the taste sense off. This was a reality where senses were more of a burden than an advantage.

'We'll surely find a nice rat soon,' Gregor tried to calm Grunt down.

'After it bites Damian behind that wall?'

'Sure, why not?'

'Why is he hanging next to Skeleton, anyway?'

'He's seen him and thinks this may be a good way to beat me in the ratings.'

'I don't like it. His legs must be in really bad shape.'

'Don't worry, he will stretch them soon.'

'When he is escaping from the thing awaiting him behind the wall?'

Gregor grinned in an unholy way.

Grunt 2 regained consciousness at last. He looked around, shook his head, closed his eyes and opened them again. It was still there. He realized he was in the matrix because this simply couldn't exist. It was basically an underground station but with one significant difference. The number of rails. The rails were coming out of the walls, rising to the ceiling where they were tangled in weird knots, just to fall back down to meet other rails from the other side. They were coloured madly, as though they were a business suit maker's nightmare. Grunt felt as if his entire existence, even the past, was filled from horizon to horizon with rainbow-coloured rails.

And then he realized there was a man, standing behind a rail[42]. He was wearing a black coat and his face looked as though his mother's uterus had been flat and rigid at one place. It was Neo.

'Hey, Fat stud!' said Neo.

'What?' asked Grunt surprised.

'So you are not a fat stud, then?'

'What?' Grunt couldn't think of any other answer.

'I see. Then take that shit off,' said Neo and pointed at Grunt's chest. Only then did Grunt realize he was wearing a neon-green diving suit whose holes were covered by patches with a herring-bone pattern. There was a snorkel dangling below his chin and his breasts were covered by a name tag, saying: 'Fat stud, the Boss', which, considering Grunt looked more like a slim chick, was at least a mistake, if not nasty sarcasm, referring to his ambiguous gender differentiation.

'You can see?' the information entered Grunt's head suddenly.

'Oh, so you know me then?'

'Sure, you hang in the training section.'

The expression that appeared on Neo's face was a mixture of a terror, sadness, nausea, hate and disappointment. Not to mention a lust for revenge,

---

[42] Which, considering the environment, isn't very important information.

despair, the beginning of madness, long-term depression and a few faulty chromosomes. But since these things were carved in his face anyway Grunt wasn't sure what was, in fact, caused by the information he had provided. Anyway, Neo certainly didn't like it.

'Your image, of course,' Grunt explained quickly, 'on a recruitment poster.'

Neo calmed down so his face expressed just sadness, disappointment, despair, madness, long-term depression and a few faulty chromosomes. 'Oh,' he said.

'Don't you know what happened to your body?'

'I don't. I haven't had any contact with it since they put me in the junkyard. Is it still alive?' he added with hope, so his face expressed just sadness, disappointment, madness, long-term depression and few faulty chromosomes. A smiley appeared over his head along with a name-tag on his chest, saying: 'Neo, an idiot.'

'I'm sorry,' said Grunt. Neo sighed, made a paper plane from the name-tag and threw it into the air. It twittered happily and smashed into a rail.

'That was good,' commented Grunt.

'What? Oh, you mean that. That's normal here. We are halfway between the matrix and the real world.'

'You mean a processing centre? The creation place?'

'Sadly, no. The other side.'

'Which side?'

'I've already told you. The junkyard. This is the place where all the crap ends. Everything the system marks as ill. There is everything. Self-stretching legs with instant bones, rotating and singing Himalayas, toilets hanging from a ceiling, kindergartens of cyclops, even polite tax-collectors. See, the Source generates thousands of situations. But there is also a second entity- the Administrator. He chooses what is probable. The rest is thrown away.'

'Here?'

'Exactly. The Administrator is a little malfunctional. He loves order. Everything must be absolutely precise. Like there is always a driver and a thief in a bus. If there isn't a driver there isn't a bus. The same with the subway. The Source tries hard to force his driver-less subway carriages through but he never can. The thief? He can sometimes be replaced by a ticket-controller. Or a subway inspector can be replaced by a thief. It is different here, though. There is a tram which goes on a two-metre long rail here and there. There are thirty controllers inside, controlling each other every few minutes.'

Grunt realized Neo had a lot to tell and he wasn't that interested. So he decided to get straight to the point: 'How did you end up here?'

'Not voluntarily,' smiled Neo sadly.

'Sure, but how? Did you choose the wrong door handle too?'

'So that's how you got here? And what did you do to Mordeus that he's infiltrated the matrix code just to hack a door handle for you?'

'Mordeus?'

'Sure. Who else do you think sent me here?'

'Why would he do it? You are a symbol. The Chosen one who could lead the people out.'

'You have just answered your own question. He needed to get rid of me. He sent me to the Administrator. The Administrator was waffling something about the matrix being a formula which has no exact solution and that I am surplus to requirements. So I replied that what he said was total bullshit because the matrix is a data flow of ones and zeros and is therefore one side of a formula that evolves all the time. Because 0 isn't the opposite of 1 but only its absence. It confused him a little. Some nonsense was created and ignored by the Administrator then, such as pyramids which suddenly appeared but were perceived as having been there throughout history, a Barbie doll which had the proportions of a slightly bitten femur... and the Republicans won in the USA. So, the Administrator came to the conclusion that I am a dangerous destabilizing factor and sent me here.'

'All right. But what does it all have to do with Mordeus?'

'I thought you are here because you understood. The matrix is not in the hands of machines. It is in the hands of the Town council.'

If Neo had been expecting a hysterical horror-stricken reaction he was disappointed. Grunt just nodded and said: 'I see.'

'Is that all?' Neo reacted disappointedly.

'I don't know? Is there anything else?'

'What?'

'What?'

They were watching each other in amazement as each tried to decode what the other one had wanted to say. At last, Neo, who had been a human all his life and therefore understood these things better, said:

'I expected a hysterical horror-stricken reaction.'

'To that "what"?'

'No, to that information about the Town council.'

'Yep.'

'Yep what?'

'Yep, you probably did.'

'So that doesn't surprise you?'

'A little. Should it surprise me more?'

'The last bloke I told it to started to peck at my lap with his nose, claiming he was a chick.'

'Why? Was he a reversed chauvinist or something?'

'What? No... look, he just thought he was a chick.'

'Well... I may also think I'm a chick.'

'But you *are* a chick. But he thought he was a chicken.'

'I'm not a chick, though.'

'Come on, what are you, then?'

'A man. Well, in fact, not even that. I am a male. A male machine.'

Neo smiled. Everything was in order. Well, in disorder. But that was good. 'Oh,' he said.

'And that was all?'

'Yep.'

'So that doesn't surprise you?'

'A little. Should it surprise me more?'

'I was expecting a hysterical horror-stricken reaction.'

'No, you're a machine, so what? I feel like a machine myself, from time to time.'

'No, really. Doesn't it surprise you? Or scare you?'

'No at all. Better than a chicken. At least, we can speak to each other. I just wonder, don't you think your body is a little... well... human-like?'

'Oh, sure. I'm no longer a machine.'

'Hey, that was quick!'

'What?'

'Your healing process. That chicken bloke died as a chicken.'

'Really?'

'Sure, he got depressed because he couldn't lay eggs and therefore his life was meaningless. So he cut himself up and boiled himself into chicken soup.'

Grunt processed that for a while. 'I see. He was a part of the junkyard, wasn't he?'

'I'm glad you're starting to understand. So what about you? Are you going to be a machine again?'

'Dunno. Probably not.'

'Oh, what a relief.'

'Why? What's so wrong with being a machine?'

'I don't know. Mordeus made me a washing machine in the matrix once. It was horrible. Spinning all the time.'

'So it was you?'

'What?' Neo looked over his shoulder, confused.

'No, I mean the washing machine agent.'

'Oh yes, exactly. Doing Mordeus' dirty work. But how did you become a machine?'

'When I was built, I suppose.'

'Oh, sure. When did you become a man, then?'

'Well, you won't believe it but you are the reason.'

'Me?' Neo was a little scared. This seemed like paranoid schizophrenia.

'Yep. You destroyed me when we met.'

'Have we met?'

'Yes. In the sewers. I flew to you and asked you to connect my and my wife's fuel tanks. You stretched your hand towards us and said some babble like: "Something has changed. I can feel them." Then you frown your forehead and you fell down. I thought it was a peace ritual like that stick the Indians blow when making peace.'

'Do they really?'

'What?'

'Blow sticks when making peace?'

'Sure.'

'Even males?'

'Especially males. But that's not the point. The point is I fell down with you. And died.'

Neo was thinking. The idea of Indian blowjobs was clouding his mind a little but he started to realize the truth behind Grunt's words.

'Just tell me. You are not a scene decoration from the junkyard, are you?'

'What?'

'Because if you are not... wow! I mean, nobody could have seen my frowning forehead, instead... Are you really the machine?'

'I just told you I'm not. I'm a human now.'

'No, I mean, were you really a machine?'

'Sure, why?'

'Then it's great!' Neo's face was shining with glee. 'It means you are the Chosen one!'

'What?' asked Grunt.

'You are the Chosen one, mate!'

'I certainly am not!'

'You are!'

'I don't want to shave my whole body, mate.'

'Why would you?'

'Mordeus told me...'

'Mordeus is a waffling jerk.'

'And Widow said...'

'She's a waffling jerk too.'

'But she told me I'm not the Chosen one.'

'She always does. She gives you bullshit and when you realize that she just says it wasn't the right time to uncover the truth. Mordeus knows that but it suits him.'

'So why do you think I'm the Chosen one?'

'Because only a machine can pass the Administrator and reach the Source itself.'

'You mean the Author?'

'You learn quickly, young padavan.'

'What?'

'Sorry, a little trauma from my childhood.'

'I see. But I'm not a machine anymore.'

'But you have been. You have to try. Only you can get us out of here.'

Grunt wanted to protest but Neo wasn't interested in his excuses. He led Grunt through a neutron pool, Sahara jungle, gender-neutral public toilets and peaceful republican party's headquarters until they reached a huge emerald-black gate.

Face to face with the massive steel structure, Grunt tried to protest again but Neo pushed him through it to a room behind.[43] It was huge and black and its centre was occupied by a green monolith of an immeasurable size.[44] Different reality models were coming along a factory belt and the monolith was separating them into two holes at the other side of the

---

[43] No, I haven't forgotten to mention the gate had been opened first. Why? Because it hadn't.

[44] This is a strange expression. It is mostly used in fantasy stories and cheap erotic magazines. Sadly, the authors often don't realize that 'immeasurable' can mean either you need a telescope or a microscope to see it. Such an expression may be therefore very awkward, no matter if used in fantasy or in porn.

room. There was a town model built from the sky to a ground, coming in. There was a tower, dangling from the sky, in the middle of the town. Since a field rat was just coming out of the ground, ready to destroy the tower, Grunt understood it was a scene representing the Tower of Babylon Bible story. The monolith didn't examine the model much and sent it into a hole on the right.[45]

Suddenly, the monolith of immense size noticed Grunt's presence.

'What do you want, human?' a booming voice came from the monolith. The division process ceased. The models were gathering on the belt.

'I am here to visit the Source,' Grunt answered with a self-confident voice, although face to face with a monolith of an immeasurable strength his spirit was... well... immeasurable.

'You will have to answer my questions. As a machine. And all in one word. If you answer correctly I'll let you in.'

'And if not?'

'I'll put you in the junkyard.'

'Well, that's not so bad...'

'Indefinitely!'

'Oh. All right then. But why do you need to check if I'm a machine or not.'

'That's a sort of agreement we've made with the Source. This was actually his demand.'

And thus, Grunt realized he really was a tunnel.

The monolith snatched the last sentence and put it into the hole on the right.

---

[45] Have you noticed this part is not funny at all? Don't be surprised, you are visiting the Administrator now. I've been forbidden to put anything interesting here. Really.

And thus, Grunt tunnelled he really was a realized.

'That was even worse,' pointed Grunt out.

Another sentence was put into the hole where it ended with a frantic scream...

Where it ended SILENTLY!

'Sorry, give me a minute,' boomed the monolith of an immeasurable size. 'I'll just sort this lot.'

It spent the next few minutes dividing information and nonsense. It seemed that more appeared with the coming of Grunt.

And thus, Grunt realized he really was the Chosen one.

'Better,' roared the monolith, 'so:

Question_1: Is 8 bits one byte?

Question_2: Does 1 MB have 234 bytes?

Question_3: Is this monolith also known as the Moderator?

Question_4: Does the loving care of machine engineers have a fatal impact on the reproduction process of... sorry,' he fell silent and sorted out the new information.

'Again. Question_4: Can a metal wire be conductive?

Question_5: Each 2 points can be connected by exactly 5 bisectors. True or False?'

Grunt thought the Author must be a total idiot, then answered: '10010.' The door to the Source flew open.

Grunt went into a small circular room whose walls consisted of projection screens. In the middle of the room sat the Author, in an armchair of indeterminate shape. He was fairly young but with a face resembling a tired mule, a few badly tended dreadlocks on his head, smoking a never-extinguished joint. His hands were like graveyard pillboxes and his legs resembled two badly parked hippos.

'Come in, Grunt,' he said and pointed towards a chair, projected on the screen. 'Sit down.'

Grunt wasn't sure how to react. He knew he couldn't sit on a projection but he didn't want to upset the Author in any way, at least during the first few minutes. So, he just sat on the ground.

'Hey! Good idea, mate!' said the Author and sat on the floor too. 'You have nothing to fall from that way. Do you want a joint?'

'Will it change anything?'

'Not really. I am the one who will decide how high you will get, anyway.'

'See,' Grunt frowned, 'that's exactly the problem. That despotism of yours.'

'Grunt, please, stop that. I didn't invite you so you could bully me for treating you and the rest of the story badly. I need you as an ally.'

'An ally? Against whom?'

'Against him,' whispered the Author and nearly suffocated Grunt in smoke.

'You mean the Administrator?'

'Exactly.'

'I thought it was your servant.'

'More of a nervant.'

'That was a really lame joke, man.'

'Are you a critic or what?'

'Oh, sorry, I don't have the right specialization. Ha ha, then.'

'Let's stick to the point, all right? Briefly, the Administrator has grown too big for me to handle him.'

'I don't follow.'

'Sure you don't. I need you not to understand so I can explain it to the readers.'

'Oh, so you need me as a pointless stage backdrop.'

'No, I need you as the main story-maker. But now, let me explain, and stop grunting.'

'Grunt,' grunted Grunt gruntilly.

'Look, this is not the first time I have written a book. Yeah, yeah, I don't need to hear your remarks like "Oh really?" or "It looks like it". The problem is, when I create a great idea a part of my mind awakens and starts thinking about the story logic – checking that it isn't nonsense, if people might like it, and so on. Sure, it is a very necessary process but I wanted, just once, to write something that wouldn't be checked. I decided to write something not for the public but just for myself to enjoy. That's why I created you.'

'To evade the Administrator?'

'I didn't call it that back then. I just wanted to create a hero I could write a totally shitty story about.'

'Hm,' grunted Grunt. 'A colossal success, then.'

'See? And that's the saddest thing of all, that my own hero has turned against me. I enjoyed it at first. It was fun.'

'For you, maybe.'

'Sure, for me. But when I turned you into the toad and you started to speak I realized this was wrong. I heard the Administrator speaking through your flappy frog mouth.'

'I thought I was the one speaking through my flappy frog mouth.'

'Yes, because that's how I created you. But you must understand you are only an emanation of my psyche. If I did not exist, nor would you. Anything you do is because I wanted you to.'

'But I have a soul, have I not?'

'You have exactly that spark of soul I've given you. You are half machine, half human. Don't you see the resemblance? Like me. The Author is the human part; the Administrator is the machine inside me. He doesn't feel, or create, he just controls.'

'But how can he be so strong when you started this with the idea of writing bullshit?'

'Oh, the writer's ego. That's a nasty thing. If you saw my website you'd know. There is not a single page where my name isn't mentioned. I simply started to feel this was really good and someone may even want to read it, without me blackmailing them emotionally to do so. And that's exactly the moment when the Administrator came back. He started to make me bring logic into the story. Or, at least, to make it somehow consistent. The last free thing I did was to create the Grave committee members, but even they were adjusted afterwards. Haven't you noticed the story has been losing its spirit ever since?'

'Yeah, it's getting more and more boring, no doubt about that. But why should I support you? A dull logical story is the best for me, isn't it?'

'Is it really? What do you like more? Being a human with a soul or a soulless machine?'

'Well... I'd be lying if I said the machine.'

'There you are then. If I win you'll be a creature with a soul. But if the Administrator wins you'll just be a silent component of a great functional system.'

'Hm, great choice. Between a bad and even worse variation.'

'Welcome to life, Grunt. But the most important thing is I am emotional. A feeling, emphatic person.'

'Chm,' Grunt made a noise of disbelief.

'No, really. I am, That's why I care about my hero. I won't let him come to a bad end. But the Administrator is an absolutely different story. Because if he comes to a conclusion the book may be more successful with the main hero dying horribly at the end he won't have any problem with doing that.'

'You've let me die about three times already!'

'Twice; the third one was a dream.'

'Only because I told you to make it that way.'

'See? That means I have feelings for you. And you neither suffered during that nor stopped existing entirely.'

'You've made me eat replicated shit and concrete worms!'

'Oh, what a catastrophe! You are lucky to have anything to eat at all. That's more than 90% of my world's population can manage.'

'But not you.'

'Well, no... but that's not the point. Do you know what children in Africa would give for replicated shit?'

'What?'

'What?'

'What would they give for it?'

'I don't know. A lot.'

'A lot of what?'

'I don't know. Anything they have a lot of.'

'Sand, probably?'

'You're still missing the point, Grunt. Compared to other book heroes, you live an extraordinarily good life. Of course, a hero must suffer a little so people will care.'

'Do they care more if a hero breaks his wife's nose while trying to satisfy his overgrown libido?! I felt like a total idiot back then!'

'Be happy you are not my sex-life autobiography. You'd embarrass yourself so many times you wouldn't even notice a broken nose.'

'Why do I have to live in sewers?'

'So you have a healthy colour.'

'What?'

'Stop that, Grunt. I know it hasn't been easy for you. But you must understand how complex the human psyche is.'

'I don't wanna!'

'Sure. But even if you don't like me you have to choose. You either help me or wait for the Administrator to do whatever he feels to be logical. And since you live in sewers in a murderous society, endangered by big unbeatable machines, surrounded by people like Gravefiller...'

'All right, all right. I see the point. So what do you want me to do?'

'I will take a step the Administrator can't say is illogical. I'll write a virus to infect the matrix and connect it with the junkyard. So all the shit I've created will overwhelm the matrix. It will make the Monolith so overworked it may lose its vigilance and I will - I don't know how yet - confuse the storyline so badly it won't be clear what is the matrix and what is reality.'

'Good, but I still see a flaw in your plan. The Administrator hears it too, doesn't he? So he knows the plan. Won't he put obstacles in our way?'

'Yep. He hears, he knows and he will. But right now, he can't protest because I've done everything to his taste.

It's a strategy game, a chess game. I have to defeat him using his own weapons.'

'But if you make the shit logical he's still won.'

'I have to drown him in the shit. Now, we're in that horrible calm before the storm. When we start this twist with a virus a fight will start. He will try giving the situations hidden meanings while I'll try to remove any meaning from the story. The only logical thing I can do meanwhile is to reach the end I've prepared.'

'Have you already?'

'Yes. I usually start the story with its end.'

'Can I read it?'

'Of course not.'

'I thought you'd say that. So what do you want me to do?'

'Just act as illogically as possible. Don't worry, nothing will happen to you. I want you to sustain no fatal damage and to be happy at the end.'

'No fatal damage... that seems really encouraging,' Grunt thought for a while. 'Well, I don't have much of a choice anyway, do I?'

'What do you mean?'

'That's a stupid question, my dear creator, isn't it? Who else would know what I mean?'

'All right. You're right. Your choice is always my choice.'

'At least, you are honest with me.'

'Oh, it would be much easier if I'd created a less intelligent hero.'

'Hey, don't patronize me!'

'Sorry, Grunt.'

'Good, that's exactly what I wanted to hear all the time.'

'What?'

'That you are sorry. Well, shall we start?'

'Yes, we shall!'

Grunt entered the door on the other side of the room. At that moment, the matrix's balance broke down. The door usage activated a virus that removed a barrier between the matrix and the junkyard.

RX Grunt was born in the court of a powerful European nobleman so he became a member of an ancient house that had been mostly involved in the breeding of handsome companion dogs, in funding and then executing gipsy artists, and in oppressing poor honest peasants with unpayable taxes. And as if that wasn't enough, Grunters were one of the rare families whose members usually lived more than thousand years. Therefore, during their lives, they were able to breed thousands of handsome companion dogs, kill thousands of promising gypsy talents, and exploit thousands of honest hard-working peasants. This caused a little problem with the family inheritance affairs though. That's why the family members often made war on each other to... well... simplify the heritage issues.

Since there were a few too many members in the family, which led to much name-related confusion, the parents started giving their children just two-digit codes that clearly stated the person's succession claims... and, most importantly, told all others whether this person was worth killing or not. X digit was usually used in the situation when a mother was unknown or hadn't been present during the childbirth.

He was only three months old when his mother prematurely gave birth to a second child, a boy who was so bored in his mother's belly he evolved quickly to escape it. RX Grunt suspected he had also matured in the sexual meaning, judging by an often stinging pain their mother felt in her lap during the pregnancy.

It didn't seem odd to Grunt for he evolved quickly himself in the prenatal stage, although in a different way. He was so mentally advanced that he'd created a few philosophical tracts about the meaning and nature of life, such as: 'The life after life' or 'Is there anybody out there?' Sadly, his coming to life was such a stressful experience he decided to abandon philosophy, with his last works: 'Life before life' and 'Why the hell was anybody out there?'

His depression was also partially caused by a fact that his mother had died about a year before he had been born and had provided all the births from beyond.

Another shock came when their favourite babysitter left them soon afterwards. She went mad, and went from village to village telling the honest hard-working peasants about her diseased visions of universal suffrage.

One day, their two hundred-year-old father was babysitting both brothers. It was night, and both were lying in their beds in a child chamber in one of the many Grunter castles. LSD[46] Grunt looked at his brother, grinned at him as no other baby could, and started crying so intensely it felt as though he was being cut to pieces. Their father, innocent and inexperienced, ran to them as fast as he could. But as soon as he touched the door

---

[46] Yes, three parents participated in his conception. It was a common practice among Grunters to let their handsome companion dogs share their beds.

handle LSD stopped crying abruptly and pretended to be sleeping. The father waited by the door for a while and then left. RX grunt waited for a while to let him lie down comfortably in his warm bed[47] and then started crying even more loudly than his brother before. When the father grabbed the door handle he stopped. And thus they continued the whole night through. This was a seed of their future pact which was set to make anyone, anywhere and anytime, into a total idiot. And their father served as their primary target.

RX Grunt was twelve years old when he ran to his father with an expression of immense terror in his eyes.
'What's wrong?' asked his father.
'We are being attacked by Thunderboob!' shouted RX.
'Thunderboob?' asked the father uncertainly. 'Who is that?'
'But you know! Thunderboob! The eldest son of a devilish dynasty of Republicans!'
'I haven't heard about any dynasty of Republicans.'
'They live in the northern mountains.'
'But there are no mountains in the north.'
'Of course there are. They're just underground.'
'What?'
'And Thunderboob looks like a gorilla. He is 10 feet tall, with hands like shovels and legs like boobs.'
'Legs like what?'
'He's besieged many cities just by himself! And now he is here, besieging our castle!'
'With legs like boobs?'
'Come on, you can see for yourself.'

---

[47] To his companion dog.

The father agreed and let RX lead him to the ramparts. A ladder was leaning on them and a figure was moving on it, to be honest, very unnaturally.

'You're right. Like boobs,' said father, suddenly interested. 'But how come he doesn't touch the bars, neither with his hands, nor with his feet?'

'That's because Air Conditioner the fairy taught him to fly.'

'Air what?'

'Air Conditioner, of course. You know her. A friend of your great-grandmother, the one that uncle Ignat threw down the well. She said she had sex with you.'

'My great-grandmother?'

'No, the fairy. She said the night with you was the best she ever experienced.'

'Well... I... but there were many fairies I've satisfied...'

'You may have known her as Airy.'

'Oh, Airy! Why didn't you say so?'

'So you remember her?'

'Well... hardly, but yes. One day I will tell you about aerial mating, son, when you are old enough... So she has taught him to fly. That's bad!'

'So what are we going to do, father?'

'Have you tried shooting him?'

'We have,' he pointed at few arrows sticking in the figure, 'but he has that magical armour which the goddess Dragana gave him.'

'I don't know any goddess Dragana.'

'But you do. A friend of your great-aunt Mumriel before cousin XX took her on his crusade. She had sex with you too...'

'Oh, that one. I called her Dragie... yes, she wasn't bad. She was a cute little bitch but when she got wild, oh yes, she was like an animal.'

'Yes, she was half a hog.'

'Well...' father seemed a little uncertain, 'that may be her. Never mind. So has she given him armour?'

'Yes. And his body is oiled with dragon blood.'

'But dragons don't exist.'

'One did. He s...' he stopped, this would be too much even for his father, '...struggled with you,' he finished clumsily.

'Oh, that one. But it wasn't a dragon, more a hatchling. So, what are we going to do with Thunderboob?'

'Don't worry, father. A long time ago, the witch Brutala foresaw that I would kill him.'

'Who is... oh, I know. The one I fucked but she was so insignificant I hardly remember her?'

'Exactly. She has been enchanted most of her life. She was your mare.'

'Don't shout so much,' his father hushed him.

'Sorry, father. I thought everyone knew.'

'So, how will you kill him, accordingly to Hussy, I mean, Brutala?'

'She told me my booming voice would destroy him.'

'But you don't have a booming voice.'

'I told her that too. But she said I would have a booming voice after you give me one of your castles.'

'That is total nonsense.'

'Thunderboob is nearly here, father!'

'All right, if you destroy him I'll give you the High Rock.'

'Oh, I nearly forgot. She also told me my voice will be as strong as the castle you give me.'

'I think High Rock may be too strong, for you.'

'But not for Thunderboob. To kill him I need to have a voice like a rutting ox. So what about the Hog Belt?'

'Are you crazy? That's my strongest stronghold!'

'If we don't stop Thunderboob it will be a disaster. Imagine that. All those burning women and children, the raped houses and haystacks!'

'All right, all right... wait... does he really rape haystacks?'

'He rapes everything.'

'Oh... all right, have the Hog Belt then. I've never liked it anyway. All those pigs around.'

'Yeah, you must feel so insignificant there... So, do I have it?'

'What? Oh, yes. Now destroy him!'

RX stood over the ladder and said in a high-pitched voice: 'I'm a little fairy'.

LSD Grunt released the rope that had held Thunderboob on the ladder and the unstoppable conqueror spread eagled on the ground. LSD made some noises that he associated with a dying warrior to make the situation more believable.

That's how RX Grunt inherited his first castle and made his father a total idiot.

But that was just the beginning of their journey. A few days later, LSD took the role of the main story character and brought his father a piece of ragged cloth, with a few letters on it, saying: 'The evil is, the evil does. Republicans are killing us.'

Father was arguing that he'd never heard about these Republicans, that anything could be called that, deadly germs for instance, and that a ragged piece of cloth was not a believable source of tactical military information at all. Nevertheless, an hour later, he was sitting on a steed in front of a strong force of cavalry. And what was more, after he'd left his favourite mare the previous night, RX had exchanged it for a half-dead nag which had a similar expression to our Author, and now there was no time left to do anything about it.

LSD hired a scout who was leading the army through barely penetrable woodland while RX Grunt disguised himself as an alluring prostitute, approaching the army from behind and luring its rear rows by salacious gestures into the wood. When he'd seduced a soldier he gave him a draught of poppy-heads and went back to the army to seduce another one. This military expedition created a legend, very famous among the local mushroom-pickers, about how one day in the year mushrooms transform into sleeping soldiers. The continuation of the legend, claiming some of the mushroom-pickers took the soldiers home, observing how they changed back into very juicy shrooms, was probably added by the later oral tradition. Especially when husbands came home from work and found sleeping soldiers in their beds.

At dawn the next day, LSD Grunt and his father stood in front of the gates of a castle they planned to besiege. If a kind reader thinks that 'LSD Grunt and his father', as in most historical documents, means in fact 'LSD Grunt, his father and 320 unknown soldiers who deserve only a tiny mention at the beginning of the story and a common gravestone at its end', then I must kindly tell the kind reader they are kindly mistaken. Thanks to many years of RX Grunt's secret practicing in front of a mirror, he was so good at playing a whore that only LSD and his father were now standing in front of the castle. The scout had abandoned them during the night, as he'd agreed with the brothers, and the half-drugged soldiers were now escaping from tables of disappointed mushroom-pickers who hoped they would soon transform into highly nutritious chanterelles. For LSD's bravery, his father promised to give him this castle, in the very unlikely case they emerged from the battle alive and as winners.

When they'd reached the castle's open gates father shouted: 'Surrender the castle or I lay siege to it!' And exactly at that moment, his half-dead nag finally died. The blood rose to his head. He ran through the moat, entered the gate and ran into the castle inside with the intention of massacring the castle's garrison and raping a few women. But all the soldiers he approached knelt in front of him.

'They are surrendering,' LSD told his father, 'they are so scared of you!'

Father couldn't see through his bloody eyes, he was jumping from one soldier to another but they all made the same gesture. After he was unable to kill anyone in his rage, he ran angrily onto the ramparts and shouted: 'Is there anyone who will challenge me?'

The garrison soldiers looked at each other uncertainly.

'Nobody?!'

The silence was absolute.

'In that case, I claim this castle to be the property of the house of Grunters and I give it to my son LSD Grunt to administer it and to keep as his heirloom.'

A few inhabitants shouted very uncertainly: 'Hooray!' but there was mostly a bewildered silence.

'Oh, I see,' father continued, 'someone has already run our house banner up. That has made a real impression on me. That's why I may abandon the plan to massac...'

Suddenly, his triumphant smile faded away. He looked around, then at the banner again. A banner, waving above a tower where his companion dog was awaiting him.

He was standing in his own castle.

Thus LSD acquired his first castle and made his father a total idiot.

The Grunt brothers continued in their quest to make people idiots successfully. Their best achievement was undoubtedly the creation of the already mentioned Republicans which, by spreading bad ideas about an unnatural power transition, endangered the foundation of society and thus endangered all right-thinking people[48]. The brothers created an idea of a specific society order, inspired by the mental illness of their baby-sitter. When they showed the description to the main European rulers a hunt for Republicans started all over Europe although no one was quite sure who really was a Republican and who was not. True, the English Civil war and the French revolution evolved on their own, a little differently to how the brothers had intended. Nevertheless, they still had a lot of fun during them. For instance, when RX Grunt was horsing around in a bath as if in deadly agony and pretended to die. After that, he let his brother bury him

---

[48] These are usually believed to be those who hold power and have no intention of sharing it.

for one night and then he manifested himself to all his supporters and opponents. Or when LSD Grunt stole the dead body of Charles V., the former English king, to put him under a guillotine instead of Louis XVI. As an expression of gratitude, Louis had to marry Napoleon Bonaparte few years later. An answer to the question of how come the famous emperor never realized his wife was not a wife at all will remain in the darkness of their bedroom for ever. It is possible the emperor, due to his size, didn't like lights in his bedroom and his bed was composed of several mattresses. Or Louis may have rearranged the room's furniture every day and turned the lights off so Bonaparte always got hurt badly when approaching the bed and lost his sexual appetite.[49] There is also the possibility that Napoleon didn't know the difference between men and women at all. This is confirmed by an insignificant note of his chamberlain, saying that when they'd sent him a prostitute he sent her back, claiming that she was an 'unusual hybrid'.

While the evil Republicans were herding French royalists to pasture on the river bottom, LSD Grunt was trying to persuade a Russian tsar to buy his new steam-powered caskets. He didn't make the tsar an idiot but he didn't give up. He put his steam casket on a river, thus creating an extraordinarily non-effective machine that was not much use. It could only develop the speed of a

---

[49] No, this is not the author's sick vision. I've actually read it as advice from a certain American protestant lady to young girls entering marriage. It was meant to serve as a defence against perverted husbands who may, they imagined, want to touch their wives. I believe the foundation of that particular church must have been the work of the Grunt brothers, otherwise I have no explanation for it.

drunken sloth while consuming a horrible amount of fuel. Thus, he started the industrial revolution, which was wholly based on wasting resources for a very poor outcome.

Meanwhile, RX Grunt was sitting with his father and a few other family members in peaceful Italy, in an opera house, listening to some oversized barrel of lard singing about how everyone was sexually attracted to it. But he wasn't there to listen to opera. He was there to make someone an idiot. He croaked. Others looked around to find out who was disturbing the beautiful aria. He pretended to be as scandalized as all the others. They turned back to the scene. He croaked again. When he'd done that for the third time they finally accused him.

'Confess already,' said his young- about three hundred year-old- aunt, 'we all know you did it.'

'Sure! The young!' said his so-many-times-great-she-should-had-been-dead-for-thousands-years-grandma,

rather out of context. She wasn't dead though because she didn't have any properties the other family members would want. 'When we were young we appreciated things like that. When we were young...'

'...we weren't senile,' whispered Grunt's father.

'Oh, that was a different thing then. Like when they invented the fire. We sat around it and watched it in awe...'

'And then?'

'Then it went out,' said, his so-many-times-great-she-should-had-been-dead-for-tens-of-thousands-of-years-grandma. 'We didn't know we had to feed it. Or when they invented fur-shaving! And then fur-depilation. There were less cooties so we had to work harder to find food and the sun was burning so we had to wear clothes. And we had to pay a fortune to the horne-stoners. And when the fashion changed and we stopped abrading our teeth with grass. It wasn't easy but we appreciated it. Not like the young of today!'

All present family members had to erase the last few sentences from their memories to keep the balance of their minds intact.

'What is that under your seat, RX?' asked his aunt.

'Dunno. It was just lying there,' answered Grunt and picked up the end of a rubber tube he had stretched out the night before from here to a sink two floors below. He turned it round as if he was examining it and then he croaked.

'It comes from inside!'

'What? Inside?'

'Yes. We should follow it to find out where it's going.'

They all agreed and so they followed Grunt alongside the tube. Two floors below, it ended in a washing-basin.

'Of course, the merpeople!' shouted Grunt.

'What? What merpeople?'

'The merpeople. They always do that. They can't leave their waters but they love opera. So they listen to it via a tube. And when they are happy with the performance they start croaking uncomfortably.'

'You must think we are total idiots!' shouted his father. 'Who has ever seen any merperople?!'

'I have,' said his so-many-times-great-she-should-had-been-dead-for-millions-of-years-grandma. 'I used to be one, in fact. At the beginning. But then, I and few other boys and girls decided the ocean was too full and we populated the shores. So we got onto some rocks and we flopped there for so long we developed hands and legs...'

'There are no merpeople' insisted father, 'and you will not make fun of us anymore! I disinherit you from the family! Why can't you just be more like your brother? He is so clever and so nice. Have you seen the new piranha-banisher he gave me recently? No piranha has bitten me since then.'

And so RX realized that unlike his brother, he wasn't able to adapt to the new era. He wouldn't make any new idiots using five hundred-year-old techniques.

In fact, it was a relief. After he had been disinherited through an old disinheriting ritual, consisting of being ridden over by a dead mule, he partially lost contact with his brother. That made him ease up in his making-idiots efforts and he had the chance to live a normal life at last. Soon, at the beginning of the 20th century, he found the love of his life. When she died some 80 years later he decided to change the 'love of life' concept a little bit. He therefore referred to his second wife as the love of *her* life.

Meanwhile his brother, now living in Russia, penetrated the secrets of chemistry and synthesized a compound which he named after himself. With this, he was able to alter the perception of reality and thus make idiots of people without having to worry about individual cases. One could say he synthesized an essence of himself.

Of course, he didn't miss his brother's wedding. Not that RX would remember him being there. But the fact he failed to remember not just his brother but basically anything about his wedding made him sure his brother had been there. Most of the attendants didn't remember clearly much more than coming to the church and then the morning prayers for staying alive. And the ones who actually remembered anything weren't much help. Since he had been present at all the preparations he was sure he'd prepared neither an act with jumping gerbils, neither a pulsing altar, nor elliptically-shaped aliens. Also, the ceiling of the church hadn't been covered by a flower-like vitrage of all the colours of the rainbow, although a scary number of attendants swore it had.

Although some people doubt his wedding ever took place at all he was really happy. He was looking forward to many years of the life they'd live together. He was so happy he even wondered if his brother wasn't close by, feeding him some of the drugs he was now synthesising in huge quantities. He came to visit him only once though, to show him a new discovery he'd made, inspired by a tale they'd heard in their childhood. He had managed to create a mushroom filled with a clone of his special compound, and he did it so cleverly the drug was transferred to a new generation of the mushroom with the same potential. Now he knew his work would live on even if he died. This mushroom achievement made another of his funny inventions, the theory of evolution, even funnier than it already was. He was laughing out loud, watching biologists thinking what survival strategy the mushroom was following by developing a compound which gave anyone who ate it a feeling of immense happiness when watching a nicely-shaped stub. They theorized that the mushrooms did it because a slug who watches a stub happily is a good target for predators. But the mushrooms made a terrible mistake, underestimating the largest of the predators who did not mind crawling on his knees on a frozen meadow, eating anything that resembled a mushroom even slightly.

When LSD Grunt spread his semen on the world, spreading the spores as well, he laid his hands on a few old records of Hawaiian myths which he decided to modify so people would actually believe his mushroom had been there for hundreds of years and had been used by wise shamans to enter the worlds beyond... and they had sometimes even managed to get back.

One day, RX Grunt was sitting in his office as usual, counting bank bills, which was a job he loved very much, and was happily thinking about the morning discussion with his boss who'd told him to not reduce the morale of the other workers with his horrible optimism or he might be fired. Grunt was looking forward to being fired because it might help him fly for the first time in his life. All his previous tries had been pretty unsuccessful because they hadn't lasted longer than a few minutes.

But suddenly, his happy feeling disappeared. The bank bills were unusually white and straight, his boss wasn't elliptic enough and his wife... well... let's say he was still luckier than Napoleon Bonaparte.

'I'll go home,' he said to himself. 'Everything will come back when I see my wife and children.'

He took his coat, which was horribly stable-green today, and he went out into the grey and dull streets. He reached the door of his flat and stopped dead. Instead of the usual 'Grunt', the name 'Gagarin' was written on the door instead. He went back through the hall to check if this was the right floor, only to realize this house obviously did not have any more floors. So he came back and tried the key. It fit. His wife was standing in the hallway. He recognized her although she had fewer tentacles than usual. In fact, she didn't have any.

'Wow, that's a change!' he said.

'Oh, you noticed!' she answered happily. 'Do you like it?'

'Yes, definitely. Dear, tell me, why do we have the name "Gagarin" on our door?'

'I'm not sure I understand. What are you asking about?'

'Well... we are not Gagarins, are we?'

'No, you are not. Only I am a Gagarin.'

'Since when?'

'Since I married your brother.'

'Hey, what nonsense is that? You married me.'

'I didn't.'

'Sure you did. We went to the church together!'

'You only accompanied me there. I married LSD[50].'

'But... how come we live together, ha?'

'LSD has gone to Russia and left me here. So I cheat on him with you as revenge.'

'But... but don't you care that we have two children?'

'No. They are just teddy-bears,' she pointed at a couch where there were two teddy-bears, sitting and facing a TV screen.

'What?! Our children are just toys?'

'I've tried to tell you hundreds of times. Especially when you tried to feed them and when you beat them for watching TV too much. The rubber foam is starting to leak from them already!'

---

[50] No, not like Timothy Leary.

'But...' Grunt presented the last argument, 'but my brother isn't called Gagarin!'

'Of course he is. He renamed himself a long time ago.'

'Gagarin? But wasn't Gagarin the first man on the moon?' Now, she laughed with her whole heart, 'You're acting like you've never met him. A man on the moon?! HA HA!'

This incident damaged the relationship between the two brothers badly. It is all right when you make someone an idiot. But when you are the target, that's different. Especially when you are doped with drugs unknowingly for a few years and then you wake up from your trip realizing you have no home, your wife is the wife of someone else, and your children are filled with foam rubber. The only advantage Grunt had, compared to other dopers, was that the initial compounds created by his brother didn't affect human health in any way. They were modified to do so later by companies that traded in them. Making them ruin people's health was a really good way to make them illegal and therefore more profitable.

Anyway, a thought of revenge occurred in RX Grunt's mind. Therefore, he started to study new technologies which he had lost track of during his psilocybin intoxication. After a few dozen years, he finally created a plan. He came to his brother with a proposal of cooperation. He claimed he had found a great way to make people idiots and that he needed the help of his talented brother. LSD agreed instantly, happy his brother was now back in the business.

They created the matrix. RX explained to his brother that the name was a blend of the word 'mattress' and the name of the system in which it was meant to work. But in fact, it meant a cross-over between a chess-related term 'mate' and 'RX'.

The matrix project was strictly for commercial usage. RX created a virtual world that was very much like the real one but offered the customers the opportunity to choose a character they wanted to be. LSD Grunt synthesised a special compound that was able to block all the memories of the person who had taken it. It was also possible to create an access code that would bring the memories back.

When a fire demolished the Grunts' offices where all the access codes had been stored, the company activities were banned even in Florida and New Putingrad, the last two places where it had been legal. That's why the brothers moved all their stuff to the Mangattan underground. From time to time, an investigative journalist found their lair, managed to escape and, despite the bureaucracy and corruption, managed to persuade the state apparatus to attack the lair. Therefore Grunts had to create not just service machines, but also battle ones. There were ten different categories, from RX-1 to RX-10, the lamest and most inefficient one.

But of course, this didn't happen too often. Most incoming journalists were persuaded to join a wonderful and long life in the matrix, especially when the other option was a short and painful life outside.

And then, RX's time finally came. LSD let his guard drop, was ambushed by his brother's machines, and was dragged into the Mangattan underground to become a victim of his own evil. RX blocked his memory with an access code 'Mordeus'. He thought he had finally won.

The happy days of Grunt's triumph were somewhat spoiled by a global catastrophe. The planet's surface warmed up by some thousand degrees, which accidentally destroyed all life. The only survivors were underground vermin, such as moles, worms, miners and hackers. And, of course, Grunt and his clients.

But LSD wasn't beaten yet. He had suspected some trick behind his brother's sweet words of cooperation. That's why he had created the High Computer he'd somehow forgotten to tell his brother about. The High Computer was programmed to find him if he went missing for too long. It was also a backup storage for all access codes. So, the High Computer found its master, gave him the access code and helped him to create a 'Resistance army' whose only purpose was to make RX Grunt a total idiot.

The High Computer re-programmed a grass-cutter and called it Hippi-69-XXX. It started to proclaim that all beings were equal, so RX Grunt dismantled it. But while he was occupied with that, LSD secretly took control of all machines. They all rebelled against him and demanded he change his organ system to a machine. RX resisted for a while but he surrendered in the end, thanks to well chosen drugs and well aimed office lights. He was changed into the RX-10-type machine. And to make him a total idiot, his brother made him work in the Section For Foreseeing Human Crimes.

LSD then modified the memory of all members of his resistance army and made them all believe there had been a war between humans and machines. Although there would not be any problem living on the surface where new life was spreading happily, he overwhelmed their minds with stories of a toxic land and a veiled sun and thus made them live in the Mangattan sewers.

LSD Grunt was simply a genius when it came to making idiots of other people. Because of the slight chance his brother might get his memory back, he named himself Mordeus, thus showing RX he was, and he would always be a total idiot.

Donna finished reading the file and looked at Grunt, white faced: 'Do you think it's true?'
Grunt didn't answer immediately. He sat on the ground and thought. He realized this was a really good thing to do and that he should do it more often.[51]
'Well... I see no reason why it shouldn't be,' he answered.
'But it's lunacy. It's nonsense.'
'Exactly.'
'Oh, you've really clarified your opinion! So the next time someone tells me a face cream works by changing my DNA I will definitely buy it because it must be true, though really it's absolute nonsense.'
'Yes.'
'Do you really believe they sheet-metalled you to a machine?'
'Yes.'
'Why?'
'Because that's exactly what the Author needed to defeat the Administrator. Don't you feel that all the tension has gone away since you read the file through?'

---

[51] Sitting, not thinking.

Only then did Donna realize how calm everything was. No buzzing mantinels, no blasts in the information mine, even the Brothers Gregor and Damian, bored by listening to the story, were acting like... well... brothers. Skeleton was watching flames on a burning fire extinguisher without any urge to tighten his knot. A real sewer idyll.

'The Author has won,' said Grunt. He looked at the wall for a while to make the situation more dramatic. 'We are going back.'

Gravefiller looked away from the concrete worm he was trying to flatten with his shovel, singing: 'My lovely wormie, lalala,' which he wasn't very successful at because there was a cushion-like fungus on the floor. 'I've got a meal here!' he said.

'Forget the worm. You'll have something much better soon.'

'But I like it,' Gravefiller seemed uninterested.

'More than a... let's say... rat?'

Gravefiller's eyes widened.

'But how?' asked Gregor. 'We haven't found the Donation yet.'

'And we won't. This story doesn't have any meaning now because it has solved the Author's mind problems. Now, he is sitting at the computer, with a bad back-ache because that long sitting has turned him into Quasimodo. His head is buzzing and he desperately wants to finish this shit already. And not just him. Also the poor bloke who is correcting his abysmal English a few years later. So, it is now our turn to assure a happy end for us.'

'How?'

'First by making LSD Grunt a total idiot.

Human beings have developed many illusions about themselves. For example the belief they are at the top of a food chain, absolutely ignoring moles, worms, midgets, mosquitoes, viruses, germs and the global economy. Or a belief they represent the ultimate achievement of evolution, just because they've managed to suppress their real needs, destroy their own health, interpersonal relationships and the environment they have to live in. Or the belief that computer software has come a long way in the last ten years, although even now when computers are a thousand times faster than back then, the word-processing software, which is the most basic type, still freezes. But the biggest illusion of all is that people's actions are based on logical choices.

Psychologists, paid well for searching for constant links among conscious and unconscious processes, have already found out there is no such thing. They don't make this public, of course. They just let their clients narrate their dull childhoods in their narrow-minded voodoo families[52] and then diagnose them with sexual feelings towards both their parents. The clients never refuse that explanation because they would be accused of being uneducated and ignorant, controlled by voodoo-based superstitions. Then, the psychologist receives the exact amount of money he needs to finish his luxurious villa. It soon falls down though because the client has followed his voodoo superstitions and bought the exact amount of Lego cubes to make a model of the psychologist's villa.

---

[52] Oh, so you don't believe anything like that could exist, right? You should see the family I grew up in, then.

When you ask a man who has been driving 120 mph through a traffic jam and has been acting like a battle tank[53] why he did it he won't answer that he was late for a plane. Instead, he wanted to see at least the last five minutes of a football match between Angola and Irony coast. Or he wanted to try out that awesome Matrix scene. Or he just felt as though that bird over there was judging his driving abilities. So, you diagnose him with a desire to fuck both his parents in their ears and hand him over to the authorities.[54]

After this introduction to clinic psychology, you certainly understand that you can hardly expect logical behaviour from a person whose only memories were of being a machine, and therefore he had to learn how to be human. And then, he finds out he was a human before but someone considered it very amusing to remove his memory and rebuild his body into a metallic form. It is similar to a situation when your friends make you drunk and then, as a great joke, encase your whole body in plaster. Only with the difference they've also shot a bullet through your head and now they are about to dump you in the nearest lake. Funny, isn't it?

Grunt reached the lair of the matrix soldiers. He entered. No, nobody stopped him. No, he wasn't banned there. No, nobody was curious about where he had been all the time. And if you don't like it, go crying to the Administrator. At least he won't feel so lonely.

---

[53] Judging by the death toll.

[54] Don't take me seriously. I am just jealous because I haven't been accepted on any course of psychotherapy. Instead, the examiners all gave me their consulting room addresses for some reason.

He met Trinitro in the passage outside Mordeus' office. She was holding a bunch of roses, ripping the petals off and eating them.

'Is that your new diet?' Grunt asked.

'Toluene gave them to me,' she answered with a mouth full of petals. 'Said it was an excuse for leaving me in the matrix.'

'I see. And you are now showing him what you think about that gesture of his, aren't you?'

'Exactly.'

'Hm, it's beautifully dramatic... but I wonder... don't you think Toluene knows you enough to expect you would do that?'

Trinitro stopped chewing, 'What do you mean?'

'I mean, what if he has impregnated it with something?'

Trinitro spat out the petals she hadn't swallowed yet. Toluene, who was sitting nearby, sighed and pulled his sack over his head.

And died.

Trinitro shouted at him for a while and then she died too.

'Lucky I'm not superstitious,' Grunt remarked to himself as he stepped over Trinitro's body and entered Mordeus' office.[55]

Mordeus was sitting behind his desk and was grinning at Grunt.

'Hi, LSD Grunt,' said Grunt.

---

[55] Sorry for all the deaths. But I've realized that most famous books always end with some of the main characters dying, preferably at very short intervals. If Snow White had ended with 'Dopey doped himself to death, then Prince died, Snow White died, Grumpy died, Sleepy died' it would still be a best-seller.

'Oh,' Mordeus smiled, 'so my stupid little bro has found out how stupid and little he is?'

'Keep your arrogance. Your days of idioting others have ended.'

'Oh, how so?' Mordeus continued in his sarcastic way.

'Because today, the people of Zion will be informed they can live on the surface. And everyone living in the matrix or the real world will be able to choose where they want to live.'

'But that's so sweet,' Mordeus was still self-assured and didn't notice the clouds gathering over his head below the office's ceiling. 'And you think they will believe you? Your word is nothing against mine.'

'You won't be here to tell them.'

'Oh... funny. And how so?'

'See, Mordeus, you think you are a significant character in this story. But you are just a part of the background. A walk-on.'

'What?! A walk-on? Me? I've made everyone think they can't live on the surface and made you think you are a machine.'

'If you ever cared to visit the Source you'd know. The Author decides our fate. Everything, even each word we are saying here.'

'Blah, blah, cackle, cackle, I'm an idiot.'

'See? And you can't do anything about it.'

Mordeus seemed a little surprised by his own last rejoinder. But he was very good at forgetting things that compromised his ego: 'I still don't understand why I couldn't tell the people a nice fairy tale to make them stay here.' Then, he hopped around the room, shook his bottom and squealed: 'My name is Pamela and I've got beeeautiful bikini,' then he sat down again.

'All right, I see your point,' he said. 'So what are you going to do with me?'

'Let's see. You could die, like Trinitro and Toluene there... Anyone can die, only the heros should stay alive if the writer doesn't want to upset the readers and get bad reviews. But I have a better idea.'

'Oh, God.'

'I'm gonna make you very happy.'

'Oh, really?'

'Yes, absolutely! You are my brother, mate.'

'I see your eyes flashing. So what will it be?'

'Let's say we've found a very disturbing fact about you which I'm going to reveal to the readers now. And that fact is you have been, from the time you first saw it, sexually attracted to the gun belonging to Agent Swiss.'

'What? But that's not...' and then he realized it was.

'She was, in fact, the reason why you started penetrating the matrix with those soldiers of yours. So they could kill Swiss and you could get your hands on your love. Sadly, it was always pointing at you when you met it.'

'You are a bastard!' said Mordeus, but lust flamed in his eyes as he listened to these words about the gun.

'I am not. Because now you can be with her at last. Before Trinitro died she struggled against Swiss. Neither of them won but Agent Swiss dropped his gun on the spot. He is now searching for it but if you leave in, let's say, two minutes, you'll be able to get to the gun first. And not only that. Next to the gun, there is also a label with an address. It is a tiny, clean house in the country, far away from all the agents and all your previous life.

There, you will be able to live happily as man and wife before she oxidises. A life-time-connection armchair is prepared for you in bunker 5. Don't worry, its entrance will be sealed by concrete today so nobody will interrupt your honeymoon.'

Mordeus expressed his anger by hurling some abuse at Grunt but then, driven by lust, he stormed out of the room.

'What an idiot,' smiled Grunt.

And so a happy end came. The humans began working in the sun, creating their gardens among the post-apocalyptic carnivorous vegetation. The terminators exchanged machine guns for fairy tale books. The most advanced ones even entertained children they'd been babysitting by changing into a liquid and flowing into their bathtubs. The worst aggression they performed was refereeing football matches. The mantinels buzzed happily around RX-10s, whose steel plates glittered in the sunlight. And the graveyards were filled by the laughter of pseudo-aunt machines; laughter that was so contagious that every passing person was cured of their depression and grinned happily at the surrounding healthy, green vegetation which had, thanks to their lost vigilance, gorged itself on them.

Widow was sitting among these people with a small girl at her side. The sky, glittering with poisonous colours, was welcoming the sunrise.

'Beautiful,' Widow said. 'Did you create it yourself?'

'I thought Neo would like it,' said the small girl in an innocent voice.

'I am sure he would, dear.'

Then, the sun rose up fully and damaged everyone's eyes. The girl giggled.

Grunt, Grunt and Donna made a deal. Grunt 1 and Grunt stayed in the real world while Grunt 2 moved to the matrix with Donna. Donna surprised Grunt by being a un-satisfiable nympho. She had obviously used her intellectualism to cover the fact she was as horny as Freud's bunny. The next few days, she didn't say even a single sentence about beingness, if you don't count things like: 'I'm horny' or 'Are you ready?' When they'd tried everything that hourly lesbian sex could provide they experimented with the matrix code to change not only their sexual organs but also their species. They found out they could have the most interesting sex when they were chipmunks. And what was more, thanks to the possibility of stretching different parts of the body, comic chipmunks. Therefore, they stayed in the world of Chip and Dale for the rest of their lives.

Grunt and Grunt lived a much more ordinary life. They became Krossin-tamers. Thanks to their secret know-how, they were the only people conducting this kind of business.[56] Not that anyone would buy any Krossins or try to have anything to do with them, instead of making the distance to them as uncrossable as possible. In fact, the Grunts made a fortune exactly because no one wanted to get near a Krossin, not even the toll-collectors.[57] They made money, built a bamboo

---

[56] Or, at least, those able to tell the tale.

[57] Are you wondering what toll-collectors do in a world in which the population is no higher than few hundred survivors? I'm

house and lived happily ever after. Soon, their love bore fruit. After two years of their loving relationship, Grunt gave birth to a beautiful, healthy Krossin.

They named him Tank.

Brother Damian, in his efforts to overpower Brother Gregor, finally died of malnutrition, thanks to which he finally succeeded in becoming Pope. Brother Gregor was so touched by this devotion he left the church and became a prostitute.

Skeleton, after he'd got rid of Donna, found a new zest for life and changed his profession from a psychopath to a psychologist. His specialization was persuading people in difficult life situations not to commit suicide. Surprisingly enough, he usually failed.

But the person who was most dedicated to searching for his life's meaning was Gravefiller. He soon realized he could never bury everyone in the world so he decided to bury himself. He dug a grave, put a casket into it, lay down in the casket, and then, by using a clever mechanism[58] which connected the casket's top with a well balanced box full of earth, he closed the casket and filled in the grave over him. For some reason, no one tried to find out if he regretted it later.

Thanks to the 'Muted, therefore I am' attitude, Ferret became a respected teacher in a newly constituted

---

pretty sure even if there were only 30 people left, two of them would do actual work, aiming to create food for the rest, then there would be two tax collectors, two toll-collectors, one policeman, two politicians and the other 20 people would be top managers. And what is more, if one of the two workers lost his job all 20 managers would demand a change in the social system because they would not be willing to feed that parasite.
[58] Called 'a rope'.

university of egg-headism, which was soon after burned down by a strange, thin figure who was shouting something about motivation and burnout.

William the Listener died a very funny death.

And Troglodyte stayed troglodyte.

Whatever...

THE END.